Bad, Bad
Darlings

Other Razorbill books by Sam Llewellyn

Little Darlings

Bad, Bad Darlings

BY

SAM LLEWELLYN

razor
bill

Bad, Bad Darlings

RAZORBILL

Published by the Penguin Group
Penguin Young Readers Group
345 Hudson Street, New York, New York 10014, U.S.A.
Penguin Group (USA) Inc., 375 Hudson Street, New York, New York 10014, U.S.A.
Penguin Group (Canada), 90 Eglinton Avenue, Suite 700, Toronto, Ontario,
Canada M4P 2Y3 (a division of Pearson Penguin Canada Inc.)
Penguin Books Ltd, 80 Strand, London WC2R 0RL, England
Penguin Ireland, 25 St Stephen's Green, Dublin 2, Ireland
(a division of Penguin Books Ltd)
Penguin Group (Australia), 250 Camberwell Road, Camberwell,
Victoria 3124, Australia (a division of Pearson Australia Group Pty Ltd)
Penguin Books India Pvt Ltd, 11 Community Centre, Panchsheel Park,
New Delhi - 110 017, India
Penguin Group (NZ), Cnr Airborne and Rosedale Roads, Albany,
Auckland 1310, New Zealand (a division of Pearson New Zealand Ltd)
Penguin Books (South Africa) (Pty) Ltd, 24 Sturdee Avenue,
Rosebank, Johannesburg 2196, South Africa

Penguin Books Ltd, Registered Offices: 80 Strand, London WC2R 0RL, England

10 9 8 7 6 5 4 3 2 1

Library of Congress Cataloging-in-Publication Data

Llewellyn, Sam, 1948–
  Bad, bad Darlings : small but deadly / Sam Llewellyn.
    p. cm.
  Summary: Shipwrecked on a tropical island, members of the Darling family find
themselves surrounded by burglers, unsavory real estate developers, and a wild boy.
  ISBN 1-59514-068-9
  [1. Adventure and adventurers—Fiction. 2. Family life—Fiction. 3. Humorous
stories.] I. Title.
PZ7.L7723Bad 2005
[Fic]—dc22

                                                                    2005023909

Printed in the United States of America

Bad, Bad
Darlings

Prologue

Nanny Buckingham was very tired, but she knew her duty. So up the stairs she trudged. The stairs were glass, full of water, with trout swimming around in them. They had cost someone a million dollars. But Nanny Buckingham was not interested in staircases and fish, however expensive. All she knew was that her feet were killing her and that she had made a terrible mistake when she crossed the Atlantic to take up employment in the Blaa de Klaa residence here in Neverglade City, looking after three of the ghastliest children in the universe.

But the self-defense instructors at the Royal and Ancient Academy of Nannies insisted that when a nanny had Made Her Bed she must Lie in It. So, ignoring the throb of bunions in her hefty brogues, Nanny Buckingham trudged on toward Destiny.

The landing was carpeted in white silk, ever so tasteful but it showed the dirt, if you asked Nanny Buckingham (nobody did). Another flight of stairs led up to the nursery floor. Nanny Buckingham cocked her ears for the howls and fighting noises that so often came down from above, the scars of old battles with bad children prickling on her skull and forearms.

Silence.

A door opened. A door closed.

Boink, said something at the top of the stairs.

Nanny Buckingham frowned. Apart from the *boink*, the silence seemed to indicate that the children were Playing Nicely. Monopoly, probably. Everyone in Neverglade seemed to spend their time buying and selling houses—

Boink . . .

—or hotels or something. And two of the daddies Nanny Buckingham knew had Gone to Jail, which was of course Not Nice. But actually Nanny Buckingham had been thinking—

Boink . . .

—that she might buy a little place herself. Just a flat where she could meet other—

Boink . . .

—nannies and have pots of tea and talk about Naughtiness and What Was the World Coming to—

Boink . . .

—when children had no manners and mummies and dad-dies were Not Interested?

Boink,

Boink,

Boink,

went the small rainbow rubber ball bouncing down the stairs from the nursery.

Nanny Buckingham's heavy brows drew together on her pockmarked forehead. Naughty, *naughty*. Balls and stairs did not mix. If she had told the wicked little lovaduck lumpkins once, she had told them a thousand times.

Suddenly Nanny Buckingham was cross, cross, *cross*. All her Nice Nanny thoughts left her. She had had it up to here with the little tykes, curse their dark hearts. The ball *boinked* toward her. She looked around to see if anyone was watch-ing. Nobody was. So, swinging back her brogue, she lined up for a mighty kick. No doubt she was thinking dark thoughts of punishment and revenge.

Reader, we shall never know.

For the ball was not a ball. It was something little Benz Blaa de Klaa had bought in the playground with his limitless pocket money and smuggled home in his platinum lunch box, because he had hoped to use it to make his brother, Otto, and his sister, Lorelei, sick. His sister, Lorelei, had recognized it for what it was. She had tiptoed across the room, not whining (for once) because she did not wish to wake Benz. Gingerly, she had taken the bright little sphere from the lunch box and rolled it out the door.

Reader, the small, bright, planet-shaped object that Nanny Buckingham was attempting to boot once and for all into space was a Mr. Skunky Atom Stink Bomb, intended to make people jump and reek.

The brogue hit the ball.

There was a flash and a truly awful smell. Automatically Nanny Buckingham leaped out of the window. She clung for a moment to a gargoyle, then dropped with a crash into the crown of a palm tree and hung, reeking and gibbering, high above the streets of Neverglade. Her brown bowler hat fell to the pavement, spun for a moment on its brim like a dropped coin, then became forever still.

Up in the nursery, the little Blaa de Klaas howled with glee.

"Silly," said Lorelei, hitting her brother playfully with a baseball bat.

"Ow!" squealed Benz.

Somewhere outside a Bengal tiger roared.

The squabbling began again.

On the day the trouble started, the Darling children were having lessons as usual in the schoolroom of the ocean liner *Kleptomanic*. Daisy (the eldest), Cassian (the middle), and Primrose (the youngest) sat in deep buttoned-leather armchairs, scribbling on clipboards. In front of them stood Dolores de Sasta, a lady burglar of Spanish extraction.

"*Bien,*" said Dolores.

"Wha?" said Cassian.

"She says the lesson is over," said Primrose.

"But there are three minutes to go," said Daisy sternly.

Dolores's scarlet smile became somewhat fixed. Teaching the little Darlings was a bit like getting sucked dry by vampires. Automatically, she began testing them on theft words.

The fine old vocabulary turned her mind to days gone by, when the *Kleptomanic* had been the lair of a promising team of burglars. But as the ship had crossed the Atlantic, things had changed. About a hundred muggers, pickpockets, and general burglars had jumped ship in the West Indies and started a burgling theme park and party space called Club Mad. Now the *Kleptomanic* was bustling at full speed toward Florida, home of millionaires, where the captain planned to turn her into a luxury hotel so the remaining burglars could Go Straight.

Dolores sighed. She did not much fancy going straight. "Let's get out of here," she said.

"¡Vamonos!" cried the children fluently.

"Excellen'," said Dolores.

The children stood up with the old-fashioned courtesy drummed into them by seventeen heavyweight nannies, one after the other. "Thank you, Dolores," they chorused politely. Then it was time for cocoa, brewed as always by Primrose, who was a genius in the kitchen. Then it was time for Free Time. Naturally Primrose went to the galley and Cassian went to the engine room. Daisy went up to the bridge.

Papa Darling was steering. Outside the windows, blue sea stretched to the horizon. To the right, or starboard, was an island covered in palms. Ahead was a little scratch of white water.

"Breakers ahead," said Daisy.

The *Kleptomanic* hummed on. By the huge brass cylinders in the engine room, Cassian and Chief Engineer Crown Prince Beowulf of Iceland (deposed) were discussing a complicated valve that was running hot. Among the great cast-iron ranges in the galley, Primrose was confecting a practice Bombe Surprise made of icing sugar, crème de menthe, and real dynamite. All over the ship, safecrackers were retraining to be barmen, burglars to be porters, and deception pests to man reception desks.

"Ahem," said Daisy, a little louder. *"Breakers ahead."*

"Don't be silly," said Papa Darling.

The *Kleptomanic*'s thousands of tons swooped and swerved to every tiny movement of the wheel in his hands. It made him feel very powerful and helped him persuade himself that he was right and everyone else was wrong. Papa Darling's gifts of persuasion had once worked on almost everyone. Nowadays the person they worked best on was himself.

They did not work at all on sandbanks.

There was a slight shudder in the floor. The *Kleptomanic* slowed and stopped. From the dining rooms far below came the jingling crash of tons of glass and china falling off wooden shelves onto metal floors.

"I told you, breakers ahead," said Daisy, folding her lips and tapping the deck with the toe of her brogue.

Just outside the right-hand window was a medium-sized

tropical island. Presumably they had run aground on a bit of it.

Papa Darling looked at his elder daughter's firm chin, accusing eye, and perfect nail polish. A sheet of sweat slid down his forehead. He looked at the place on his wrist where in the days of his richness a gold Rolex had gleamed. "Goodness, is that the time?" he mumbled, and slid away into the depths of the ship.

Daisy sighed. It had been a long, strange trip to this sandbank from the ruins of the Darlings' incredibly luxurious home at Númro Uno, Avenue Marshal Posh. It need never have happened. Indeed, it would not have happened if Papa Darling had been less interested in jewels and holidays and paving over nature preserves. If he had not been interested in all that, the Darlings would have spent more time being a happy family, and AAA Aardvark Child Minding and Security would never have existed, and there would have been no ship and no Sleepy Cake, and the piano in Avenue Marshal Posh would never have been detuned—

Wait a minute. We are going too fast. What, you will be asking yourself, is he going on about? Why does he not tell me who all these people are, get the facts in order, and start telling this story with everything in the right sequence?

Dear reader, you have got a point. The reader always does. Fasten your seat belt. Cabin staff, seats for takeoff.

Here we go.

The Darling children, Daisy, Cassian, and Primrose, had arrived aboard the Bad Ship *Kleptomanic* when they had followed a burglar after he had entered their luxury home disguised as a nanny. The captain of the *Kleptomanic* had turned out to be their long-lost mother. Her chief assistant was the kindly but plain-speaking burglar Pete Fryer. The crew consisted of more burglars and the mad chief engineer, who had once been Crown Prince Beowulf of Iceland. After a pitched battle with White Van Dan and his villainous Builders, the *Kleptomanic* had sailed across the Atlantic, picking up Papa Darling, the children's father and the captain's ex-husband, who had been marooned on a desert island by Mrs. Secretary Darling, his second wife. Papa had been given a chance to improve his personality by cleaning the ship's lavatories. It would not be true to say he was happy about this.

The captain was kind, musical, chic, adventurous, and just about everything else you could want in a mother. If she had a fault, it was a tendency to look on the Bright Side. As I have pointed out, she had decided to turn the ship into a luxury hotel. Soon, everyone would be Going Straight and living happily ever after.

Clear? Well, then.

Just now the captain was one of the party on the bridge of the completely stuck *Kleptomanic*. The warm breeze was ruffling her midnight blue, silk sheath dress and she was looking on the bright side with the help of a powerful telescope.

"A tropical island!" she cried. "Such a charming one, too, and uninhabited by the look of it!"

"But the ship is jammed good and proper on the bottom of the sea," said Pete Fryer.

"And we may never get off," said Cassian, who had been looking up the tides in a large blue almanac.

"Details, details," said the captain vaguely. "Time for a swim."

Pete blew into a voice pipe and passed the word to Daisy Darling, who passed it to Primrose, who passed it to Chef, who passed it to Dolores de Sasta, who passed it to Giant Luggage, who passed it to the chief engineer, who told his teddy bear. In the end the tidings reached the lower-deck lavatories, where Papa Darling was having a meeting with the gloomy ex-safecracker Dismal Eddie, now his executive assistant.

"Dismal," Papa was saying, "we have an agreement, am I right or am I right?"

"You are right," said Dismal. "I do your job cleaning the lavatories. And you will pay me a lot of money when your money arrives."

"And you are responding brilliantly to this delegation situation," said Papa Darling hastily.

"But what I want to know," said Dismal, "is how this person sending money is going to know your address."

"Make your mind easy on that score, my good man," said Papa Darling. "I would pay you cash right now, except I have left my wallet in my other suit."

"You haven't got another suit," said Dismal doggedly. "I wants it *now*."

"Perfectly reasonable," said Papa. "But quite imposs . . ."

His voice died away. The ship was suddenly full of cheers and running feet. Through the lavatory porthole he saw boats rowing happy ex-burglars to a beach of the purest white sand. Some were already swimming. Others were beginning sand castles. He noticed Dismal's bloodhound face lit with wonder alongside his at the porthole.

"Cor," said Dismal.

"Oi!" said Papa.

"You can take your job and shove it," said Dismal. "I'm off swimming." He galloped away.

Papa Darling shook his head, heaved a sigh at the frankly disgusting toilet before him, and reached for the rubber gloves.

"Yee ha!" cried Nosy Clanger, zooming past like an excited bee. "Bet there'f treafure!"

Papa Darling curled a lip at the tiny moron and started to mop diligently. As he mopped, his mind was far away.

His old company, Darling Gigantic, had flattened mountains, filled in lakes, made nasty untidy waterfalls run down lovely neat pipes, and won awards for paving over nature preserves. On these tidy gray surfaces DG had built thousands of houses out of cardboard and plastic foam, which they had then sold for billions.

Those days were behind him now, of course. He had promised the captain and his children. But Nosy Clanger had set strange currents running in Papa Darling's mind. Little by little, a picture was forming.

The picture was of this tropical island, but not fringed with white sand and green with coconut palms. Oh, no. On Papa Darling's mental movie screen the beaches had become paved roads thick with cars, beside which people sold other people table lamps made out of seashells and T-shirts that said THEY WENT TO PARADISE AND ALL THEY SENT ME WAS THIS LOUSY T-SHIRT. There were hundreds of squat concrete apartment buildings and the fuming chimneys of a fertilizer factory. Over the whole mucky shambles soared a huge white concrete tower with a neon sign that said HOTEL DARLING GIGANTIC TROPICANA. Among the buildings thronged thousands of tourists with ghastly shorts and open wallets. . . .

Papa Darling found that his mouth was watering like a loo flushing. He mopped on, mind churning.

For a red-hot business executive like Papa Darling, every island was a treasure island. It was just a matter of finding the right approach.

The Darling children were sitting on deck chairs on the bridge, sipping ice-cream sodas made by Primrose and watching the busy scene. A committee of children and burglars had provisionally named the island Skeleton Cay. Now the children watched the throngs of burglars dressed in striped bathing suits cavorting in the waves.

The captain joined them. "Having a lovely time?" she said.

"It will be nice when we get off this silly sandbank," said Daisy.

The captain glanced at Cassian from under her great lashes.

Cassian said, "I fear that may not be possible."

"Why on earth not?" said Daisy.

"We're hard aground at the top of the highest tide of the year," said Cassian. "So, basically, we have no chance of moving until next year."

"Next *year*?" said Daisy.

"If then," said the captain, passing her beautifully manicured hand across her noble brow. "The ship . . . well, Cassian?"

"Bad," said Cassian, looking nautical. "Ships are meant to float on water, not sit on land. Bulkheads numbers one to thirteen are already showing hairline cracks. We have drilled arrester holes, but it is worrying, very—"

"Say what?" said Primrose.

"I think what dear Cassian is driving at in his sweetly technical way," said the captain, "is that the dear old *Kleptomanic* is collapsing under her own weight."

"In layman's terms," said Cassian.

Silence fell, broken only by the infectious rhythm of the captain's cocktail shaker and the distant cries of the beach frolickers.

Finally Daisy said, "So we need another ship."

"There was a time when we did not have one at all," said the captain.

"But you get used to having things," said Cassian.

"Particularly ships," said Primrose.

"How true," said the captain.

More silence, heavy with deep thinking.

"Meanwhile," said the captain, "perhaps one should explore the island."

"We'll take care of that," said Daisy.

"Thank you, *thank* you," said the captain.

"*De nada,*" said Primrose.

Three drinking straws roared as one.

The Darling children went ashore in one of the ship's boats. As they explored the coastal regions, Cassian made an accurate sketch map. When it was finished, the three Darlings sat on a rock by a waterfall. Primrose handed out drinking coconuts and they considered what Cassian had drawn.

Round the edges of the island were coconut groves fringed with beaches of purest silver. Above the coconut groves rose a small but nicely formed mountain, its domed summit dented with hollows that looked not unlike the eyes and mouth of a skull. From one of the skull's eyes rose a wisp of smoke. The river by which they were sitting ran from the skull's mouth, bounded over various waterfalls, and arrived in a swamp. In the swamp lay things that looked like fallen trees.

Cassian, watching closely, noticed one of the trees open a mouth full of sharp teeth. "Alligators," he said.

"How shocking," said Daisy. "Up the mountain!"

They had been walking for ten minutes when Primrose cried, "Look!"

They looked. A small brown figure flitted across the hillside, stopped, glared at them, and went bounding away through the woods as fast as it could run.

"A wild boy!" said Primrose, hands clasped.

"Indeed," said Daisy, who did not altogether approve of wildness.

"Apparently you quite often get them on tropical islands," said Cassian. "Living on roots and berries mostly."

"Yuck. Poor boy!" said Primrose, her heart melting like butter in a frying pan over moderate heat.

"Up the mountain!" cried Daisy impatiently.

Up the mountain they went.

As they scaled the slopes, plucking a papaya here, a passion flower there, the eye sockets of the skull-summit revealed themselves as caves. Underneath the left-hand cave was an odd structure.

"A ladder," said Cassian.

Frankly, this place did not entirely have the look of a wild island. Wildish, to be sure, but not untrodden by human foot. There was the ladder. There was also the path, edged with small stones, heading upward, and the little flight of steps leading to the elegant white picket fence, and the notice on the gate on the picket fence that said NO HAWKERS NO CIRCULARS NO TOURISTS. SO FAR AND NO FARTHER. YOU HAVE BEEN WARNED.

"We are none of the above," said Daisy, sniffing. She trotted up the steps and pushed the gate. It sprang open. A sign on its back said DUCK OR GROUSE.

"What is this, a menu?" said Primrose. "Argh."

This "argh" was produced by her brother, Cassian, who had grasped both his sisters and hurled them behind an overhang of rock. Just in time, for over their heads thundered a mighty avalanche of boulders. On the first one, Daisy was shocked to notice, someone had painted the words SO LONG, SUCKERS.

"*Well*," said Daisy, sitting up, dusting grit from her hair, and putting her hands on her hips.

She marched up the mountain, followed by her brother and sister. Sure enough, at the bottom of the skull-shaped summit was a shiny blue door. Next to it was a bellpull. Under the bellpull was a brass plate bearing the words GO AWAY.

Daisy did not approve of landslides or rude notices. She was not in a frame of mind to go anywhere except where she wished to go. Seizing the bellpull in both hands, she gave it a smart heave.

From inside the mountain's summit came the tolling of a great bell. The tolling died. Silence swept in. Out of the silence grew the sound of feet, shuffling. The door opened with a creak of hinges. An eye appeared.

"Good afternoon," said Daisy politely. "We are sorry to trouble you, but we would like to talk about your island."

"Talk?" said an ancient voice.

"Our ship is wrecked here," said Daisy. "We'd like to stay for a bit, if that's all right."

"Ship?" said the voice.

"Quite a big one," said Cassian.

The door swung open all the way. Standing inside it was an ancient man. His hair was long and wispy, his eyes were wild, and he was wearing a three-piece suit of moldy linen.

"Come in," he said.

The children looked at each other.

"Let's go," said Primrose.

He led them up a dusty staircase and into a room lined with ancient books and pictures.

Daisy made the introductions with all due ceremony. "And who," she said, "are you?"

The old man sat down with a crackle of knee joints. "Bit

hazy on that," he said. "All I know is my name is Quimby and I came here a long time ago, to think. And I thought a lot, but then I kept getting interrupted by people, so I arranged the Home Landslide to sweep them away. Works pretty well, but it is awful hard work putting the boulders back. So the thinking stopped. And you are the first strangers with decent manners I have met for . . . well, quite some time."

"What were you thinking *about*?" said Cassian.

"Thinking. That is to say, thinking about thinking."

"A philosopher?" said Primrose.

The ancient eyes lit up like car headlights. "Yes!" he cried. "Yesss! It all comes back to me! I am Eustace Quimby, Professor of Philosophy at the University of Neverglade, and I thank you for introducing yourselves and recalling me to myself. Yet . . . how do I know?" He fell silent.

"Huh?" said Primrose.

"Know what?" said Cassian.

"Know you exist," said Professor Quimby. He shook his head, as if to clear it. "I am sick to death of this island," he said. "You have no idea how much trouble it is getting rid of—well, no matter, no matter. How I wish I were somewhere with glass windows, pizza close at hand, and lots of maintenance staff." He looked up sharply. "How much will you give me for it?"

"Give you?"

"I'd like to sell it to you. You have kind faces."

There was a short, astonished silence. Then Daisy, feigning stupidity, said, "We are only children, of course, but I expect our captain—Mummy—would give you a bag of silver and gold."

"A big one," said Primrose.

"Fairly big, anyway," said Cassian, always the careful type.

"Enough to buy something very modern and nice," said Daisy.

The professor beamed. Then his face clouded again. "But how do I know you exist? One cannot make deals with mere figments."

They all thought deeply. Then Primrose said, "Where's the kitchen?"

The kitchen was small and dirty, with a round window looking toward the west. Primrose put her fingertips together and swept the shelves with her mild blue eyes. Ingredients combined and sizzled in her mind.

She stopped.

Outside the window, on the blue sea beyond the green flanks of the island, a boat had come into view. Inside, there was a telescope. Primrose climbed onto a box and peered into the eyepiece. The boat was dark gray, with black glass windows that gave it a blind, sinister look. It was hurtling across the water, towing a white arrowhead of spray.

Heading, unless Primrose was much mistaken (she practically never was), for the beaches of the wreckage of the *Kleptomanic*.

The boat slowed and lay bobbing in the sea. A hatch on top opened. A head came out and examined the world through binoculars. The hatch closed. The boat turned round, accelerated, and roared back the way it had come.

Exactly, thought Primrose, as if it had been on the way into the lagoon, had seen the *Kleptomanic*, and had changed its mind.

Odd.

But not nearly as important as cooking.

Primrose reached for the eggs. There was a skillful blur of hands, a cloud of flour, a clatter of pans. Then she was trotting into the study, carrying a plate on which teetered a golden stack of pancakes.

"Slight lack of basic ingredients," she said. "Tell me what you think."

The professor folded a pancake in his fingers and popped it into his mouth. An expression of cosmic bliss spread across his ancient features. "Mmmmm," he said. "Delicious. Too delicious for me to have invented. So they exist. And if the pancakes exist, the world exists. And so do you, and so does our deal!"

"Exactly," said Primrose.

"Have another," said Daisy politely.

The professor polished off the stack, becoming more convinced by the minute. He took a piece of ancient paper from a pile on the table, dipped a quill pen in some violet ink, and scribbled a note.

"Here!" he cried. "I hereby yield to you the island! On condition, of course, of no paving! This paper is your proof!"

Cassian looked at the writing. *Bill of sale,* it said. *I hereby give to the Darlings my island in return for one bag of silver and gold, medium size. Signed, Eustace Quimby, professor.*

"We'd better take this to the captain," he said. He turned it over. "It seems to have a map on the back."

"Has it? Oh, well," said the professor, who seemed keen to leave. "Right! Let's go!"

They trooped down the mountain, picking their way over the remains of the Home Landslide. There was a movement among the boulders.

"The wild boy!" cried Primrose.

"That's no wild boy—that's my grandson, Dean," said the professor.

"He ran away," said Daisy.

The professor's ancient face became grim. "Perhaps he thought you were someone else."

There was no time to ask who, because Dean the Wild Boy was in their midst. He had freckles, a brilliant white smile, and a firm handshake.

"Hi, y'all," he cried with infectious enthusiasm. "How's it going?"

"Great," said Primrose. Wild or not, he was just about the most marvelous thing she had ever seen.

"I have sold the island to these good people," said the professor. "I'll be off when I've picked up the money."

"Wow!" cried Dean the Wild Boy, his white smile practically meeting at the back of his head. "Fantastic!"

Daisy found this odd. It cannot be pleasant, she reflected, for one's grandfather to sell one's tropical island home from under one's feet. So why all the grinning?

"Will you stay with us?" said Primrose. "We may need your local knowledge."

Dean the Wild Boy looked uncertain.

"Please," said Primrose, fixing him with her mild blue eyes.

Dean the Wild Boy's face cleared. "Sure!" he cried. "Sure thing!"

Normally such warmth would have made the Darlings suspect someone was trying to take advantage of them. But Dean the Wild Boy's was a deep, rich, heartwarming all-American model, and it left no room at all for suspicion.

On the *Kleptomanic*'s bridge, the captain was delighted with the deal. She locked the bill of sale in the ship's safe. They said an affectionate farewell to the professor. A small boat was filled with precious metals, and he rowed it over the horizon, happy as a clam.

"Just as well there was a cooking fire going," said Daisy.

"There wasn't," said Primrose.

"How did you make the pancakes?" said Cassian.

"There was an electric ring," said Primrose. "And a sort of windmill thing."

"Wind generator," said Cassian. "Bank of salvaged submarine batteries, probably, hooked up to an inverter."

"Quite right," said Dean the Wild Boy with a new respect.

Cassian allowed his eyes to rest on the top of the dome, from which a wisp of gray smoke still floated into the air. It was all very interesting. Very interesting indeed.

"Now, if you have quite finished gossiping," said the captain, "may I remind you that we need to make a plan so we can get a new ship and carry on with our lives?"

All that afternoon, boats shuttled between ship and shore. In the evening, the ship's company ate Primrose's conch chowder at long tables, following it with three-chocolate ice cream, washed down with a choice of Horlicks malt beverage or Ribena to drink, both new to Dean the Wild Boy and both pronounced by him delicious. The sun sank. Night fell: a thick, tropic night, black as velvet, sewn with diamond stars.

The captain sighed. "So beautiful," she said.

"His master's," said Pete Fryer, close by her side as always.

"Sorry?"

"His master's voice, very choice."

"Ah."

Daisy's eye tracked the silver zip of a meteorite to the horizon. A horizon, now that she came to look at it, glowing strangely red. But sunset was long gone.

"Over there," she said. "It's a city."

"Neverglade," said Dean the Wild Boy.

"Never heard of it," said Daisy.

"Sunny place. Lots of millionaires."

"Hmmm," said the captain. She mused for a moment. "I think we may have to put off Going Straight for a bit. Yes, indeed. Neverglade sounds like our kind of town."

Later that night in the children's stateroom, Daisy held a meeting of Primrose, Cassian, and Dean the Wild Boy. Dean the Wild Boy told the others about his life. He had been brought up by his grandfather since infancy.

"I am real glad you came," he said. "Tropical islands are all very well, but they get lonesome."

"How strange to live here," said Daisy.

"It was okay at first," said Dean the Wild Boy. "I guess Grandpa thought I'd turn into a Noble Savage."

"What's one of them?" said Primrose.

"Someone not fat, not mean, not messed up by garbage TV. Grandpa reckons that humans are basically good, turned bad by the complications of life."

"Goodness," said Daisy.

"Poor you!" said Primrose.

"Weird," said Cassian.

Daisy had a thoughtful look in her eye. "So are there many children in Neverglade who are—*ahem*—fat and mean and messed up by garbage TV?"

"Same as anywhere else," said Dean the Wild Boy.

"Lots, then," said Daisy.

Primrose was watching her sister intently. "Daisy," she said, "you are thinking something."

"Yes, indeed," said Daisy.

"What?" said Cassian, blunt as always.

"Well," said Daisy, "it is very nice doing lessons and all that. But . . . well, I sort of miss nannying."

"And burglary," said Primrose.

"Or we could live here on the island and sort of fix it up," said Cassian.

Dean the Wild Boy's brilliant smile vanished. He looked nervously over his shoulder. He said, "You should ask yourself, why did my grandpa sell the island so quick and cheap?"

"Because Primrose convinced him he existed, using pancakes," said Cassian.

"Uh-uh," said Dean the Wild Boy, shaking his mop of tow-colored hair. "Maybe he sold it because he knew someone was coming to take it away." He had gone pale beneath his tan. "I have to go to bed now."

"Wait," said Primrose. Her mind went back to the kitchen of Professor Quimby's cave house. A dark gray boat with black windows floated into her mind. "Who was going to take it away?"

"Can't say," said Dean the Wild Boy.

"You must," said Daisy.

"Leave it, Daise," said Primrose protectively.

"Very well," said Daisy. "But do not think I will not make further inquiries. Now, gather round, all. I have an idea."

The Darlings and Dean went into a huddle. She explained.

"Votes?" she said.

"Aye," said Cassian.

"Aye," said Primrose.

"Yeah. Um, aye," said Dean the Wild Boy.

Daisy then went and discussed a few things with the captain, who was at her daily piano practice. After that they all went to bed.

The beds were splendid four-posters, but nobody slept very well. As the tide went out, the *Kleptomanic* made groaning, buckling noises. In the morning, the porthole glass was cracked.

"What's happening?" said Primrose.

"We have a race on our hands," said Cassian. "A race against time."

"How pompous!" said Daisy.

"How true!" said Primrose.

"How weird!" said Dean the Wild Boy, now almost one of the family.

After breakfast, the loudspeakers summoned the ship's company to the theater for an emergency meeting. Everyone was there, except Papa Darling, who was cleaning a blocked toilet on H deck with long rubber gloves and a sullen air.

On the stage stood the captain, ravishing in a raw silk suit by Chanel. Beside her stood Daisy in full hot-weather nanny regalia—green lightweight overalls with tropical white bowler hat cover, sportbrogues, pool cue pointer in hand.

"Good morning, mates!" cried the captain.

"Good morning, Captain and Nanny Daisy!" chorused the ship's company.

The uniform took them back to their glory days, when they had been burglars who made their entry to the scene of a crime by disguising themselves as nannies.

"Now, then," said the captain, "I shall be brief. Map calculations show that the great city of Neverglade is a mere thirty miles away. Unfortunately, our poor old *Kleptomanic* is falling to bits. So bang go our plans for going straight and luxury hotels. I know we all agree on the need for a new ship. To get a new ship, we need to integrate ourselves with the community—"

"Pardon?" said a voice.

"Or, in other words, to get into the houses of the posh,"

said the captain. "I am informed that there are plenty of spoiled brats in Neverglade. We need to meet a few of the worst and richest. So we are going to open a Brat Camp."

"Wha?"

"A place where bad children can come and be trained to be good," continued the captain. "It will be called Camp Civility. Daisy, over to you if you would be so kind."

Daisy settled her bowler firmly on her head and flipped page one of her chart. "Camp Civility will be aimed at the type of person shown here—" Daisy rapped with her pool cue pointer on the top bit of a bar graph, colored gold and labeled MILLIONAIRES. "We will use the camp to select families of the precise kind shown here." She tapped with her cue on another chart, topped with sparkly gold stars and marked MULTIMILLIONAIRES WITH EXTRA-BIG YACHTS. "We go to their houses in nanny gear. We scout the locations of safes and spoons. You know the rest."

"Hooray!" cried the ex-burglars, and they set to work with a will.

By lunchtime, the *Kleptomanic*'s punishment cells had been removed from the ship and erected in a coconut grove. A teddy bear had been arranged in the corner, curtains bearing a design of sweet bunnies hung over the heavily barred portholes, and a small, dirty kitchenette erected next door and stocked with oatmeal and custard powder.

"There," said Pete Fryer to Daisy, who had removed her brogues and was wiggling her toes in the sand. "What do you think?"

Daisy pursed her lips nannyishly. "Ghastly," she said. "Hideously uncomfortable. Just right."

Burglars are good workers in an emergency, and Camp Civility grew fast. They used the pillars from the first-class saloon and the ranges from the galleys and made an attractive coffee table from the wheel. Two days later, the emergency arrived.

By the afternoon, a thick gray smudge of cloud crept in from the east and a low swell was rumbling on the sandbank. Chief Engineer Beowulf was standing by a huge pile of gear, ticking off items on a clipboard.

"How's it going?" said Cassian.

The chief turned. His bear, the Royal Edward, was buttoned into his jacket to protect it from the drizzle. "Goot," he said. "But schtorm comink."

Cassian nodded. The chief had been brought up in Iceland and held the coveted order of the Codfish and Volcano. What he did not know about bad weather was not worth knowing.

All that evening the wind rose. By suppertime the waves were breaking big and heavy round the ship.

Like all Icelanders, the chief loved a wreck. "Goink tonight," he said, doing a mad, lumbering two-step. "Goink right to bottom of sea. Hee, hee!"

The sun went down in a brief, watery smear of pink. Night fell—not a jeweled vault this time, but a damp black blanket that tasted of salt. The Darling children and Dean the Wild Boy made up beds under a roof of palm fronds.

All night the wind howled and moaned, and the sea roared, and from the blackness of the bay came a great din of booming and crumpling.

When Cassian woke, the wind had dropped. The sea was a sheet of blue glass. A thin plume of smoke floated straight up from Skull Mountain's right eye. It was as if the storm had never been, except for one thing.

Yesterday the *Kleptomanic* had been a hulking black shape on the sandbank.

This morning the *Kleptomanic* was gone.

In the days that followed, Cassian converted two of the ship's lifeboats into small but attractive steam launches. From time to time, enormous boats from the mainland sailed into the lagoon, many of them carrying brawling knots of children. All were politely turned away by one of the steam launches, whose crew issued them discreet cards on which was written in looping script:

CAMP CIVILITY—
CHILD CONVERSIONS
WOODWORK, WELDING, RESPECT FOR ELDERS A SPECIALITY
GALA OPENING
TUESDAY (INFORMAL DRESS)
BRING A FRIEND

Tuesday dawned bright and clear, with a tiny breeze that rustled the coconut fronds and swelled the sails of the fleet of yachts crawling out from the mainland. At the entrance to the anchorage, Cassian stood on the steam launch, directing traffic. His gold-braided tropical uniform shone in the sun, and Daisy had removed all but the worst grease stains from his face.

Anchors rattled down. Soon dozens of yachts lay like swans in the green reflections of the trees. Lifeboats manned by teams of burglars rowed the guests ashore and into Camp Civility's conference center, where I hope, dear reader, you will join them.

The conference center consisted of the fixtures and fittings of the *Kleptomanic*'s theater transferred to a charming clearing in the palm trees. The red velvet seats groaned under the mighty bottoms of many millionaires, who sobbed with joy as Daisy lectured them on politeness and applauded wildly at the end.

Outside the tent, Primrose was having an excellent morning at the stoves among the trees. Flaming pans lit her mild blue eyes, and her sauces were turning out creamy and triumphant. She loved to see everyone tucking in to her snacks—particularly Dean the Wild Boy, who, Primrose reckoned, needed feeding up. Through the steam of his fourth helping of chili con carne she saw Cassian's figure out in the lagoon. His white-uniformed arm was up and he was waving a boat to an anchorage.

The boat howled into view. Its wake drenched Cassian's Number One uniform. It thundered in toward the land, hit the beach with a bang, and lay there smoking. It was dark gray and dangerous-looking, with black windows. Small men in dark suits spilled onto the beach.

Primrose turned her eye back on Dean the Wild Boy. He had gone as white as the beach sand, which was as white as chalk, if not whiter. "What's wrong?" she said, full of doubts about her chili.

"It's him," said Dean the Wild Boy between bloodless lips.

"Him?" said Primrose, flooded with relief that the chili was fine. "Who?"

"Don't ask!" hollered Dean the Wild Boy, hiding behind the stove.

A man and a small boy climbed out of the dark gray boat, allowed themselves to be helped ashore by the men in dark suits, and strutted up the beach as if they owned it.

When Primrose looked around, all that remained of Dean the Wild Boy were the deep marks of running feet.

A couple of minutes later, Cassian came squelching up the beach, soaked to the skin. The owner of the dark gray boat was leaning against a palm trunk, smoking a thin cigar, with a seen-it-all-before look in his eye. There was a thin child near him, wearing dark glasses and hacking messily at a coconut tree with a skinning knife the size of a sword.

Something about the pair said to Cassian that these were not your normal millionaires. Normal millionaires were fat and noisy. This man was thin and quiet, like a snake. The boy was thin, too, with palm tree hair, dark glasses, and the family venomous look.

Cassian shrugged out of his uniform and hung it up to dry by the cooking stoves. Under it he was wearing a T-shirt and baggy shorts. He wandered through the palms toward the thin man and said in a high, feeble voice, "Hello, nice kind man, I have lost my mummy."

The man raised an eyebrow the same thickness as his little black mustache. "Tough," he said.

"But can you help me, please, Mr. Man?"

"God helps them who help themselves," said the thin man, spitting impressively out of the side of his mouth. "It's root, hog, or die in this world, muchacho, and quite right, too. Alone we came into this life, alone we will leave it."

"So you can't help me?"

"Help? Tchah," said the thin man, grinning a grin that

showed a diamond in one of his front teeth. "You'll make out. Or not. Not my problem."

"Oh," said Cassian. "What is your name, Mr. Man?"

"They call me Gomez Elegante," said the man. "Eef they not too scared to say my name at all. And this ees my son, Gomez Chico. Remember the face. Now go, trudge."

"Wha?"

"Hop it. Scram. Take a powder. Get from here. Vamoose. Do I got to paint a picture?"

"What he ees trying to tell you ees, get lost," said the thin child from behind its shades.

But Cassian had already gone, jinking through the trees, heading for the nursery.

Here Dean the Wild Boy's freckled face and sun-bleached mop of hair appeared cautiously from behind a tree. "Did he leave?" Dean the Wild Boy hissed.

"Who?"

"Him."

"You mean Gomez El—"

"Don't say it!" hissed Dean the Wild Boy, eyes spinning with terror.

"Eleg—"

"Nooooo!" moaned Dean the Wild Boy, and was gone again, his bare feet drumming on the sand.

So Gomez Elegante had the suit of a millionaire, and the shoes of a millionaire, and a mustache that Cassian planned to copy as soon as possible. But he did not have the *atmosphere* of a millionaire. Frankly, he seemed much more like a burglar, but without the warmheartedness and sense of fun that made burglars such great people to be with.

Cassian decided that he would keep an eye on Gomez Elegante. He had lunch, then sallied forth again. The crowd was watching an exhibition of Polo for Tots staged by two pygmy horse thieves.

And there were Gomez Elegante and his son, still in the shadows. Gomez Chico was pulling the legs off an ant. There was a man with Gomez Senior, deep in conversation. A man dressed in green gum boots and an apron with a pair of rubber gloves in the pocket. A man very familiar to Cassian: Papa Darling, past CEO of Darling Gigantic, superintendent of the ship's lavs. Papa Darling looked very interested in what Señor Gomez was saying.

Which was odd, because the only thing that really interested Papa Darling was money.

The sun sank in the west. The guests went home. The inspection parties jogged round the island, cleaning up. The little in-patients were snoring safely behind the nursery bars. It looked like it would be a beautiful evening.

When the intelligent reader spots a phrase like this, it is clear that there is trouble on the way. Reader, you are highly intelligent and spot on. Dark clouds were gathering.

Soon the storm would break.

• • •

An inspection party flung open the door of the Camp Civility lavatories. Immediately it flung the door shut again and leaped back, coughing and gasping.

"What is it?" said Primrose sweetly.

The inspection party stopped coughing long enough to wipe its streaming eyes. "It is . . . That is to say, miss, it is *none too clean*."

"How awful!" cried Primrose.

The captain glided up on her kitten heels. "Let me look!" she cried. She stood framed in the low doorway, unblinking. "Where," she said mildly, "is Papa Darling?"

They passed the word. No word came back. They searched the whole island. No trace of Papa Darling could be found.

"Where can he be?" said the captain.

Cassian stepped forward. "He was talking to a Mr. Gomez Ele—"

"Don't say that name!" shrieked Dean the Wild Boy.

"And actually," said Primrose, "I saw them sharing a joke."

"So perhaps they have gone off together," said Daisy.

All four children watched the captain. She sighed, as if over a wayward burglar. She sat down and reached moodily for a cocktail shaker. "Perhaps I pushed him too hard," she said.

"Wha?" said Primrose.

"His dignity. Perhaps it was unfair, all that lavatory cleaning. He has undoubtedly run away."

"Naughty, I call it," said Daisy, and pursed her lips.

The captain shook her head and put her hand on Daisy's. "There is right, and there is wrong, and there is the place where we all live, which is somewhere between the two," she said. "You will learn."

Later the sound of the piano floated across the lagoon. The captain was playing the low-down blues.

"There is something *about* the captain," said Daisy, scowling at her fingernails.

"Tell me about it," said Primrose, scowling at hers.

"She is our mother," said Cassian.

"Ye-es," said Daisy. "But what does that *mean*?"

"The reproductive process is a fascinating thing," said Cassian. "Take, say, a bird. Or a bee. Then—"

"Tch," said his sisters, diverting their scowls from fingernails to brother. "Don't you *understand*?"

"Understand what?" said Cassian.

"Listen," said Primrose. "Papa has done a runner and the captain is upset. Right?"

"But she made him clean the toilets," said Cassian.

"Which he deserved," said Daisy.

"S'pose," said Cassian. "But I'm not surprised he's gone. I would have. Wouldn't you?"

"Honestly!" said his sisters, together, then they folded their arms and gazed stonily in opposite directions.

Cassian felt somewhat uncomfortable, as he always did

in the presence of things without cogs, pistons, or boilers.

"Beats me what she sees in him, though," said Primrose eventually. "I mean, Pete's a way nicer guy."

"Papa is the father of the captain's children—i.e., us," said Daisy. "This is an awesome responsibility." She repursed her lips. There was a short silence, of the kind that happens after someone has dropped a very big cannonball onto a very small frog. "We must go and look for him. Dean, you are very quiet."

"If your papa has gone off with . . . a certain person, we should all keep quiet," said Dean the Wild Boy. "If we wanna keep breathing." He wandered off, apparently deep in thought.

Primrose watched him go. She frowned. Then she wandered after him.

She stayed back, keeping out of sight. She watched him walk up the mountain, over the remains of the Home Landslide, and up the steps to the door of his grandfather's mountaintop apartment. The door hung half open. He went in.

Primrose did a bit more frowning. Perhaps he was missing his grandpa, poor wild boy. But then again, perhaps not.

She climbed the steps and walked through the door.

All the books had been pulled off the shelves. The contents of the kitchen cupboards lay scattered on the kitchen floor. The windows were broken, the curtains pulled down. The sofa cushions were inside out and springs coiled from the mattresses.

"What a mess!" she said.

"Who's that?" said Dean's voice, high and scared.

"Me," said Primrose.

"Phew!" said Dean the Wild Boy, with a relief that warmed Primrose's heart.

She went up the rest of the stairs. Dean the Wild Boy was sitting on what was left of a chair, his head in his hands.

"What is it?" she said.

"He's got it," said Dean the Wild Boy in a strange, far-away voice.

"Got what?"

"What he always wanted."

"What who wanted?"

"Gomez El—nooooo!" cried Dean the Wild Boy. "He'll hear me! His name must not be spoken! Curse him! Curse—"

"Oh, for goodness' sake, of course he won't hear anyone say anything," said Primrose firmly. "He left in his nasty stinkpot with his revolting child. Now, can the cursing, Dean, and come back and I will make you some cocoa and you can tell me all about it when you have calmed down."

Dean the Wild Boy went back, drank the cocoa, and did indeed seem to calm down. But of the wreckage and Gomez Elegante he would say no further word at all.

Next morning, a speedboat roared over the horizon, came to a halt in the lagoon, and a serf in a snow-white sailor's uniform carried a crested envelope to the captain. She visited the Darling children and Dean the Wild Boy as they were eating their breakfast.

"I have received a message from someone called Blaa de Klaa," she said. "A baroness, by all accounts. Apparently their nanny jumped out of the window and something ate her. The baroness requests our help."

"Of course we can," said Daisy.

"Too right," said Primrose.

"And I'll start the hunt for a boat," said Cassian.

"And while we're at the Blaa de Klaas'," said Daisy, "we will track down Papa."

"You'd better take Nanny Pete, just in case," said the Captain.

"Dean the Wild Boy will help, too," said Primrose. "Won't you, Dean?"

But Dean the Wild Boy's place was empty. They searched high and low—none higher or lower than poor sad Primrose. But Dean the Wild Boy was utterly, utterly gone.

The sign over the office of Hiram Fish said HIRAM FISH
USED NET AND TRAWLER. Hiram Fish was at his desk, barking
into a telephone. "So the boat sank?" he said. "So I should
maybe boist into tears? So what we have here is a situation
where the buyer should beware."

Muffled yelling came from the far end of the line.

"So you want your money back. Sure. So I have a big, big
tank of shahks that need feeding. So if you want, come over
here to get your money, but my safe is in the middle of the
shahk pool and"—here his voice became a snaky hiss—"*the
shahks are hungry*. So listen here, you sonofa—"

Here the door opened and two strangers walked in. One
was very tall and somewhat stout, with sad brown eyes that

43

had a strange whirling movement. The other was very young and very short, with dark hair growing low over a grease-stained forehead and eyes like twin power-drills. The big one, Hiram was surprised to notice, had a teddy bear buttoned into his tunic. Hiram's first thought was, How the hell did they get in? Then he noticed his secretary, Irma, bound and gagged in her chair, and realized it was all quite straightforward. So he smiled, revealing sixty-three teeth, all of a dazzling whiteness, and made room for his second and third thoughts, which were, How much money do these people have? and, How can I get my hands on all of it, very soon?

The smaller of the two people spoke. "We have a lot of money and it is all in this bag," he said, rattling a shopping bag in his right hand. "We need a boat."

"Trawler," said the teddy bear man. "Vantink large excellent trawler."

"Well, well," said Hiram, showing thirty extra teeth. "You guys sure have come to the right place. Here at Hiram Fish Used Net and Trawler we sell used nets and trawlers. What you see is what you get, eh, shipmates?"

"You vill kindly address me as Chief Your Highness," said the teddy bear man haughtily. "And this is Engineer Cassian."

Hiram rose smoothly to his feet. "Well, Your, er, Majesty, we will now go take a look at some boats. You can leave your money here. We will take care of it for you."

They walked out into the light, toward the line of trawlers rotting on the lot. Hiram noticed that Cassian was still carrying the money. Well, that was to be expected. It was a hard life, running a used-trawler lot. Luckily, Hiram was a hard man.

Or so he had thought till now.

From the sea, the Blaa de Klaa residence was a great white block of marble knee-deep in palm trees. The converted ship's lifeboat, *Polite Children*, came smoothly alongside the private quay. Nosy Clanger, trim in his sailor's uniform and with his tattoos polished to a high sheen, attached bow and stern lines and pushed out a smart gangway. The nannies shouldered the ditty bags containing essential nanny gear. Then they stepped onto the quay, smallest first.

"Tara, ven," said Able Seaman Clanger, grinning toothlessly.

A security man who had been snoozing in a hut by the quay woke with a start. "Hey!" he cried. "Who you?"

"We are the nannies," said Daisy.

"Got no instructions," said the security man.

Daisy's nose went right up in the air. "That is a problem for you and nobody else."

"Ooh," said the man, in an offensively relaxed manner. "But what I got here is folks called, lemme see, Camp Civility Outreach, right?"

"Aye, aye," said Nanny Pete.

"Okay. You carryin'?"

"Only our ditty bags."

"I mean weapons."

"Certainly *not*," said Daisy. "We are Kind but Firm, and that is all."

"Huh," said the security man. "I hope Mr. Mortician got your measurements. You like snakes?"

Daisy's smile became a little strained. She hated snakes.

"And insects. You know them little stingin' spiders that kill you dead?"

"Intimately, thank you," said Daisy.

"Well, she got them, but big," said the man.

"Yuck!" murmured Primrose. She was still rather quiet since the disappearance of Dean the Wild Boy. And she absolutely hated spiders.

"Well," said Daisy, "nice as this is, we can't stand around chatting all day. Nannies, forward!"

"Oh, yeah!" cried the voice behind them. "I forgot. They got big cats, too!"

"Tabbies?" said Nanny Pete.

"Bengal tigers," said the black man.

"Can't abide cats," said Pete.

"Well, well," said Daisy. "What will we do?"

"We will Make the Best of Things!" chorused the other two nannies.

They dumped their luggage in the luxurious nanny flat. They assembled various personal items in their ditty bags.

"Lead on," said Daisy.

Pete led on.

The children's wing was a splendid building, based on a Greek temple, with French windows onto a terrace and a frieze of sweet Winnie-the-Pooh mosaics. On the terrace at the foot of the steps up to the entrance door, fragments of broken bottle glittered in the Neverglade sun and a childish hand had put spectacles and rude bits on Pooh, Eeyore, and Piglet. From within came the sound of metal music.

The nannies trudged up the steps in the glaring noon. On the platform at the top, they saw that someone had left a pair of filthy sneakers on the marble paving.

"Oh, dear." Daisy sighed wearily.

"Pull the other one—it's got bells on," said Primrose.

Nanny Pete stumped over to the sneakers and trod firmly on each of them with his size-fourteen brogues. Then, having checked carefully for hidden wires, he picked them up and shook them one by one. Bits of scorpion pattered onto the paving. "You'd think we was born yesterday," he said, scowling. "Onward!"

As they walked through the big bronze doors, the metal music stopped, leaving a deep, thick silence. There was a sort of anteroom, with high windows glazed with yellow glass.

The windows were obscured with something that might have been net curtains. They were not net curtains, though.

They were spiderwebs.

As the nannies peered into the dimness, they realized that all around them there were hundreds of other eyes peering back.

"Ooooh," said Primrose.

"It's all right," said Daisy, rummaging in her ditty bag and pulling out a large spray gun. "Bugs, begone!" she cried, pumping away at the wooden handle.

The eyes went out. There was a mass trampling of tiny insect feet, followed by thin screams from the garden, where various security guards were discovering the dark side of entomology.

"We are obviously dealing with intelligent children," said Primrose.

"Highly creditable," said Daisy, through lips stiff with nerves.

They went through the next door. Here the light was a series of beams creeping in through little round windows in the temple dome. On the floor was a most unpleasant dry rustling.

"Gulp!" said Daisy.

"*One* minute," said Primrose, pulling from her ditty bag a cake tin.

Daisy felt something slide round her ankle. It slid all the

way round, squeezed, then carried on toward her knee. It was heavy and coldish. Even through her thick nanny tights she could feel it was scaly. It stopped at knee level, perhaps to get its breath, and started to make a noise like a leaky bicycle tire.

"Something is crawling up my leg," said Daisy, in a voice as thin and sharp as a razor blade.

"One of them shivers," said Pete.

"Shivers?" said Primrose.

"Shivers and shakes, snakes," snapped Daisy. "Now, would you please get it *off* me?"

"Where's your nanny nerve, sis?" cried Primrose bracingly.

There was the sound of someone pulling the lid off a cake tin and of softish objects hitting the floor.

"What's that?" said Daisy, through chattering teeth.

"Mice."

"Mice?"

"Special mice," said Primrose. "Essence of mouse, to be exact. With suet, cement, and the merest pinch of spent uranium."

"Never mind feeding them, will you just get *rid* of them?"

"Ten seconds," said Primrose.

With something that was probably a cobra wrapped around her knee, waiting was all Daisy was going to do. Then she was going to run and run and run and—

The band round her knee loosened. There was a soft thump and a slither. Then there was a creak and a gulping noise.

Primrose struck a match on the seat of her nanny skirt. She said, "They'll sleep for months."

There were about thirty snakes on the ground. Daisy recognized them from her *Every Girl's Book of Deadly Serpents*. They were king cobras, mostly, with a sprinkling of diamondback rattlers and tiny but deadly krait. They all had bulges in the middle and seemed extremely sleepy. When Pete prodded one with his toe, it moaned faintly and burped.

Daisy summoned up the remains of her courage. "Onward!" she cried.

On the far side of a door, something cried back. Except that this was not so much of a cry as a coughing roar.

"Oops," said Pete, sounding tight-lipped. "I'm allergic."

Daisy strode briskly to the door and turned the handle.

This room was not dark at all. It was a sort of conservatory, with a glass ceiling through which the tropical sun streamed with furious intensity. Full-sized trees grew from the muddy ground, their branches tangled with creepers. The air was hot and wet and thick with the smell of cats. The reason for the smell stood nose to nose with Daisy. It was a tiger the size of a horse, black lips writhing back from its fangs in a frightful snarl.

"Puss, puss," said Daisy.

"I am going to sneeze," said Nanny Pete faintly. "I just know I am."

Daisy said, "Poor you. Here is a hanky," and passed him one embroidered with little skulls and crossbones by Primrose's busy needle.

The tiger seemed to be tensing itself to spring.

"Er, Primrose?"

"Oops," said Primrose. "Thinking about something else."

From her ditty bag she extracted a bunch of greenish gray vegetation, which she handed to Daisy. Daisy thrust it forward. The tiger opened its mouth and snarled at her with teeth ten centimeters long. Then it smelled the leaves. Its eyes crossed and it slumped sideways, purring foolishly.

"Wha?" said Nanny Pete. "A-*choo*. 'Scuse me."

"Bless you," said Primrose.

"Wha . . . *choo*?" said Pete.

"Catnip," said Primrose. "Gidgy gidgy gidgy." She tickled the tiger's vast belly and it wriggled with pleasure.

"When you have quite finished playing with the animals," said Daisy, "there is work to do."

Briskly she led her fellow nannies through the jungle to the door at the far end, twisted the handle, and walked through.

Beyond the door were glass stairs with the trout swimming in them. At the top of the stairs was a playroom, from which came the sound of heavy squabbling. Around the playroom walls stood an industrial-sized stereo, a whole-wall home cinema, and several motorcycles. Everything was broken. Three children slouched among the wreckage. Each of them had a baggy T-shirt, baggy jeans, and greasy shoulder-length hair. They were staring at the nannies in total horror.

"But you're *dead*," they chorused.

"Are we?" said Daisy. "Dearie me. Now, then. Who is going to clean up this mess?"

"Don't know," said the middle-sized child. "Don't care."

"You will start now," said Daisy.

"And when you have finished," said Primrose, "I will give you supper."

"Very nice it will be, too," said Nanny Pete, twinkling roguishly.

The smallest of the children took a step forward. "My brother and sister cannot be bothered with such orders," it said. "We Blaa de Klaas are descended from the Perhapsburgs, you know—the ruling family of just about everywhere since time just about began. No Perhapsburg in history has tidied up a room. Ever. It is an idea so far beneath us that we cannot see it with a remotely controlled submersible."

"Not even one fitted with closed-circuit TV," said the eldest one.

"Until now," said Daisy.

The child frowned. "I beg your pardon?"

"Welcome to Planet Nanny," said Daisy. "On which you will tidy your room. And on which you will eat up the nice supper that Primrose cooks."

The child smiled a superior, tolerant smile. "Incorrect," it said.

Daisy sighed. "Primrose?" she said.

Primrose stepped forward with a tray on which lay three tiny pies. She said, "Try these, O most serene and illustrious of children."

"If we must," said the eldest, who (Daisy had noticed) had a rather greedy face.

The other children reached languidly for one each, popped them in their aristocratic yaps, crunched, and chewed.

And stood very still.

Daisy walked along the line of scruffs. She was a lot shorter than them. The faces above her did not so much as flicker.

She turned to Primrose. "What have you put in them this time?"

"Eggs. Sugar. Cornflakes. Chocolate."

"No eye of newt? Black cat bone?"

Primrose drew herself up to her full four-foot nine. "Nothing unusual. What you see here is a simple Deliciousness Trance."

"Wha?"

"These poor children have for so long eaten the blandest of foods, beefed up with sugar and chili, that *really delicious* tastes just simply blow them away."

"Goodness me!" said Daisy.

"One of them moved," said Primrose.

A sort of primitive awareness was indeed returning to the eyes of the Blaa de Klaas. They looked around them for more cakes.

"Now then, children," said Nanny Daisy. "Names?"

"Otto, Benz, and Lorelei. Where are more liddle buns?"

"Later. First, to work."

"Work? What means that?" said Lorelei.

"If you do as you are told, I will explain."

The little Blaa de Klaas frowned. "Told?"

"Listen. You do what we ask with regard to donating snakes and tigers to zoos and playing exciting board games while tidily dressed." Daisy leaned forward, her eyes hypnotic beneath the rim of her bowler. "If you do this, Primrose makes you more cakes. If you no do this, Primrose no make no cakes."

Light gleamed in pasty faces. "Cakes like the last ones?" said Lorelei.

"More delicious than the last ones," said Primrose.

"Impossible," said Lorelei, who seemed to be the spokesgirl. She mused. "So when you say, 'Jump!,' Nanny Daisy, you can now expect us to ask, 'How high?'"

"Attagirl," said Primrose.

"As long," said Lorelei, "as the cakes keep coming."

At Hiram Fish Used Net and Trawler, things were turning ugly. Chief Engineer Crown Prince Beowulf of Iceland (deposed) seemed to be finding it difficult to concentrate. "Vot do you call zis?" he said, wrinkling his almost endless nose.

"Shrimp trawler," said Hiram Fish, waving a hand at the pile of stinking rust hanging from its mooring lines by the quay. "One lady owner, fishin' only for personal amusement. Nice boat, attractive price."

"Aha," said the chief, not really there. "Cassian?"

"I'll just kick the tires," said Cassian.

"Not too hard," said Hiram, grinning the grin of a chimpanzee with extra teeth and an anvil on its foot. "A bit—"

But Cassian had skipped lightly onto the deck. He had slid down the ladder into the hold. From his coat pocket he had pulled a hammer. "Yee ha," he said, raising the hammer above his head and bringing it down with a terrible thwack on the trawler's hull. There was a dull crunch. The head of the hammer went straight through. A geyser of water leaped from the rotten plating. Cassian scooted back onto the quay. "I could be wrong," he said, "but I think this boat is sinking."

"Built very light," said Hiram dully. "For speed."

"Und much rusty," said the chief absently. "Next?"

The next boat had an engine that caught fire when (against Hiram's advice) they started it up. The one after that was made of wood and Cassian poked his finger straight through the rotten hull. There was another and another. By the sixth boat, a pall of smoke hung over the yard and Gobstopper-sized lumps of muscle were working at the corners of Hiram Fish's jaw. His entire staff was putting out fires and pumping out boats holed by Cassian's deadly hammer. A couple of trawlers had sunk to the bottom of the harbor.

"Step this way, gennelmen," said Hiram, sweat running down his scarlet face.

"Sure," said Cassian, following him to the middle of the dock. "And?"

"Stand right there," said Hiram, indicating a red X on the boards.

"Why?"

"I wish to take your photograph."

"Why?"

This was a question nobody had ever asked before. In Hiram's experience, everyone loved having his photograph taken. "It's nice to have your picture took," he said.

"So show us how it's done," said Cassian, eyes wide with childish curiosity.

Hiram had had enough of these extremely awkward customers. Furious, he stamped toward the red X. "You stand here," he said. "What is the problem?"

"No problem," said Cassian.

Probably if Hiram Fish had not been in such a rage, he would have remembered that he had been carefully standing in front of a notice that said DANGER—SHAHK POOL. Cassian put out a thumb and pressed the red button below the writing.

"No

   o

      o!" cried Hiram as twin trapdoors opened under
   his feet and he plummeted into the shahk pool.

"Yes," said Cassian, peering with interest at the arrange-
ment of used-boat salesman and triangular fins. He rum-
maged in his pocket and tossed a couple of little packets into
the inky water.

"Shark repellent, I suppose?" said the chief, as if he did
not really care.

"Ketchup," said Cassian.

Deep in thought, they climbed down the ladder to the
steam launch and set off. The sound of very fast swimming
rose from the shahk pool. Amusing as this might be, it was
no way to find a new ship. They would have to look for a better method.

"Madam," said Daisy, "we must have a party."

The Baroness Blaa de Klaa was an exceedingly thin
woman, tanned to the color of Swiss milk chocolate, her spi-
dery hands crusted with enormous jewels.

"Party?" she said, eyeing this really very small nanny from
under false eyelashes like medium-sized furry animals. "Vot
business of yours?"

"A children's party," said Daisy. "Children are my business."

"Vot children?"

"*Your* children."

"Vot, are they still here?"

"And very nicely behaved they are nowadays."

Daisy clapped. In marched the little Blaa de Klaas. Their hair was neatly cut. They were dressed in khaki shorts, polo shirts, and pith helmets. Their faces shone with happiness and the joy of cooking. They were discussing a chess problem in low, eager voices.

"Who is zis?" said the baroness.

"Your children, madam. We were speaking of them earlier."

The baroness stalked over to the children, who raised their helmets politely. She frowned at each face. *"Donner und Blitzen!"* she hissed. *"Mirac'!"* She rounded on Daisy. "How did you do this? Are you a vitch?"

"They did it themselves," said Daisy. "Thanks to haircuts, followed by the introduction of more appropriate pets—i.e., sweet bunnies—regular meals of excellent food, amusing games and stories, a little welding and bricklaying, and early bed. What do you think of it, children?"

"We love it, Nana," said the aristobrats in chorus.

"Specially the cakes," said one of them.

"Hee, hee," said the other two, wriggling.

"But you are makink them *ordinary children*," said the baroness.

"There is no such thing," said Daisy. "Now. The party. We will need names and addresses for the invitations."

"Zo," said the baroness. She strode to a shelf, plucked out a volume, and tossed it to Nanny Pete, who caught it cleverly. "All is here."

"What is it?" said Pete, scowling.

"The Blue Book," said the Baroness, "containing the names of everyone that the children are allowed to meet, no rubbish, no time wasters." She plunked into her chair. "So get to it, chop chop."

"Come, children!" cried Daisy, after a slight pause for astonishment. "We are going to have *such* fun!"

Daisy leafed through the Blue Book. Papa could be with any one of these staggeringly rich people. She was looking forward to having a really good ask around.

All that day they pasted bunny pictures onto invitations while the coughing roars of the Bengal tigers echoed in the shrubberies. The invitations were sent out that evening. The replies came back by return of post. Everyone would love to come on Wednesday next, it now being Wednesday this.

Early on Saturday morning, a feather of smoke was seen on the southern horizon, and there was the *Kleptomanic*'s steam launch, *Polite Children*, come to take Daisy and Primrose for their day off. Nanny Pete, who was to remain behind, stood on the quay waving a spotted hanky as the launch vanished toward Skeleton Cay. As soon as they were out of sight of land, Daisy took off her hat and began polishing her nails a pretty bloodred. Free at last!

The day-off nannies chugged happily toward the island. They overtook two small men with beards and ponytails paddling a canoe. The top of Skull Mountain popped over the horizon, leaking its wisp of smoke. Then came the lower slopes, and the roofs of Camp Civility among the green fronds of the coconut grove, and the music of the piano drifting across the lagoon.

As Daisy and Primrose threaded the columns of the great hall, Cassian joined them. His hands were deep in his pockets, his brow thick with oil.

"Captain's not quite herself," he said.

"How would you know?" said Daisy, who, besides having a low opinion of her brother's emotional insight, was still suffering the remaining shreds of nanny mode.

"Ask yourself, what tune is she playing?" said Primrose, who had been listening.

Daisy listened. It was "Stormy Monday."

The Darling children marched forward.

"'The eagle flies on Sunday,'" sang the captain, sweet and low. "'Saturday is just the same. Oh, the eagle flies'—hello, children. How lovely to see you." She did indeed look pleased. But Daisy thought she saw in the great dark eyes a sadness beyond words. "How were things ashore?"

Daisy gave her report and the captain's beautiful features arranged themselves into an expression of radiant delight.

"A *party*!" she said. "How *lovely*! And how is Pete?"

"Diamond geezer," said Primrose.

"Quite right, quite right," said the captain. Her face grew grave. "And your father?"

"Nothing."

The captain reached into her highly desirable Moschino handbag and took out a long mauve envelope. "This arrived, though."

She passed it over and Daisy read it aloud: "'Unavoidably detained elsewhere with regard to a business opportunity that has presented itself. I feel it imperative careerwise to pursue all options on offer re: upward mobility issues. Ciao, baby. Papa Darling.' What on earth does *that* mean?"

Primrose said, "He has gone on the run because scrubbing lavatories makes him sick."

"Quite," said the captain, drawing a heartrending arpeggio from the piano keys. "And you can bet that he has plans and that no good will come of them." She played a large minor chord. "Oh, how I love the simple life of this island! The lacy shadows of the palms, the coconut milk so delicious with rum and green curaçao! But how I wish we had a ship! And how I wish that Pete was here!"

"The ship will come," said Cassian. "We have not found the right one, but we have a plan." He scowled. "Only . . ."

"Only?"

"Nothing."

"Spit it out," said the captain.

"I can't seem to get the chief to, well, *concentrate*."

"What's wrong?"

"He's been building a sort of hut on the mountain. Won't let anyone near it. Not that anyone wants to. Stinks of rotten fish." He pointed a grubby finger out of the window. "Up there."

High on a shoulder of Skull Mountain was perched a little wooden house. There was a smaller house next door. Both houses had pillars on the front and a rather grand look.

"Tiny palaces," said the captain fondly. "The smaller of the two will be for the Royal Edward, one suspects."

"Palaces with a clothesline outside the front door."

The captain picked up a telescope. "Not a clothesline," she said. "Cod drying. A little piece of Iceland on Skeleton Cay. Hence the fish reek."

"He's been taking machinery up there all week," said Cassian.

"Bless him," said the captain absently. "Now do tell me, Daisy, I'm sure Cassian's plan is lovely, but what's yours?"

Daisy began to explain.

Primrose sat turning the envelope over in her blunt cook's fingers. She raised it to her nose and sniffed deeply. "Patchouli," she said. "Hint of gardenia. Aviation fuel."

". . . so once the Blue Book children have been to the Blaa de Klaas' party," said Daisy, "we will make our inquiries about Papa. From what I have seen of Neverglade, it seems the sort of place where a crooked real-estate person will feel very much at home."

"I fear you may be right," said the captain. "But don't get too involved. All we want is a new ship, and perhaps the contents of half a dozen tip-top safes, and to get out of here."

"And Papa?"

"We want him back, of course," said the captain.

"What for?" said Daisy, amazed.

"To teach him a lesson," said the captain. "*What* is that noise?"

A yelling and roaring had broken out in the hall. "Far from refined," said Daisy, or at least that is what we must assume she said, for the actual words were drowned in a grand splintering as the door burst open and into the room thundered a tight ball of fighting humanity.

"Ahem!" said the captain, in a discreet but piercing voice.

The ball immediately separated into its parts. There was Giant Luggage, standing with his scarred knuckles brushing the floor. There was Nosy Clanger, his many tattoos glowing with excitement. And there were two small men in cutoff jeans, SAVE THE ALLIGATOR T-shirts, ponytails, and beards, soaking wet.

"What is going on?" said the captain.

"Hur, hur," said Giant Luggage (this was all Giant Luggage ever said).

"Bese great big oaphs," said Nosey Clanger. "Pound 'em in a canoe. Fnoofing."

"He means snooping," said Primrose absentmindedly. She was staring at the ponytail man on the right. She stepped forward and gave the beard a sharp tug. It came away. She gave the ponytail a yank. It came away, too, revealing the tow-colored hair and bronzed face of—

"Dean the Wild Boy!" cried Primrose.

"But what are you doing, sneaking around dressed up like this?" said Cassian.

"It's so lovely to *see* you!" cried Primrose, hugging him.

"We wanted to see what you were doin'," said Dean.

"But you know perfectly well," said the captain.

"I know what you say," said Dean the Wild Boy. "But that's not necessarily what you do. Tell 'em, Omar."

"Ahem," said the ponytail man, his Adam's apple leaping nervously about in his neck. "My name is Omar Careful and I am active with the Marigold Binkschneider Foundation, among whose objectives are—"

"Cut to the chase, Omar," said Primrose out of the side of her little pink mouth.

Careful went red. "It has lately been brought to our attention—"

Careful's eyes lashed once round the room, saw no escape,

and returned to his feet. "Okay," he said. "I have information that you plan to convert this island—"

"Skeleton Cay," said the captain.

"—Skeleton Cay into a concrete tourist resort, with a casino, high-rise hotel, and fertilizer factory complex."

"I fear you have been misled," said the captain. "As you can see, our only plan is to dedicate ourselves to the appreciation of the finer things in life and the care of our many palm trees."

"That's not what the guy said."

"The guy?"

"The guy at the inaugural meeting of Colossal Realty."

"The guy who was here," said Dean the Wild Boy. "The guy who was cleaning the restrooms. We saw him. At the meeting. In the Hotel Splendide."

There was a small, deep silence.

"Talked like he was maybe English," said Careful. "Foreign accent anyway."

"English people do not have foreign accents," said Daisy through pursed lips.

"This one did, and so do you," said Careful. "Fact, come to think of it, he looked kinda like you. And he had a note saying Professor Quimby had sold him the island."

The Darlings looked at each other. All four of them said, "Papa!"

"Excuse me," said the captain, who had gone rather pale.

She left the room. When she came back, she was even paler. "My safe," she said. "The lock has been picked. The paper Professor Quimby gave us is gone."

"Papa could not pick a lock to save his life."

"Uh-oh," said Primrose. "You have to ask yourself, who was his assistant on the toilet patrol?"

"McMurtrie," said the Captain.

"Would that be Dismal Eddie McMurtrie?" said Cassian.

"Yes."

"Otherwise known as No Safe Is Safe from Safecracker Dismal Eddie McMurtrie?"

"That's the one," the captain said and sat down suddenly on the piano stool.

"So Papa can sell the island. And any minute now, someone is probably going to arrive and start paving over Skeleton Cay," said Daisy.

"That was certainly the plan as expressed at the meeting," said Careful.

"Which makes it all the more urgent to find Papa and make him give that bit of paper back," said Daisy.

"Must we?" said the captain.

"Of course we must," said everyone in the room except the captain (and, naturally, Giant Luggage).

"Well," said Primrose. Then, to Dean the Wild Boy, "Had any lunch?"

"No."

"Well, I'll cook you some if you teach me how to paddle your canoe."

Dean the Wild Boy looked at her. Then he broke into his dazzling smile. "Gee, it's great to be back," he said.

So everyone went canoeing and swimming, and all too soon it was time to climb into nanny gear and start back for the mainland.

As the *Polite Children* glided across the lagoon, the shore party saw Dean the Wild Boy waving from the beach and heard the ripple of the piano through the pillars of Camp Civility. The music rose through the palm fronds and the wheeling tropical birds, past the weird clankings coming from the chief's little piece of Iceland, and drifted away to sea, mixed with the wisp of smoke from the cooking fire in Skull Mountain.

Though come to think of it, there was still no cooking fire on Skull Mountain. Never had been, as far as anyone knew.

Odd.

Wednesday was party day.

Reader, it would be pleasant to describe the glittering contents of each party bag, the tactical ebb and flow of each game of Musical Chairs, Pass the Parcel, and Simon Says. Reader, life is not pleasure but deadly earnest. So we will pass over the details, cutting swiftly to the chase.

It was a costume party. The Children of the Blue Book were disguised as a couple of baseball teams, some clowns, several girl skating champions, and one extremely lonely roll of lavatory paper. While Nanny Pete supervised the games, the Darling children were able to pump the other nannies for information about their papa.

These mighty women sat bolt upright on hard chairs,

bowler hats yanked firmly down over beetling brows, chins bristling. Daisy circulated with the teapot, asking insinuating questions. "Yes," said an Alp of a woman apparently called Nanny Anvil. "We are the Hotburgs. We are frankly very noble and in shipping. No, we have never met a Papa Darling."

"Excuse me," said Daisy.

A girl skating champion had got hold of the end of the lavatory paper disguise and was zooming across the room with it. Smoke was pouring from the lavatory paper child's spinning toes. Dashing a bucket of water over the charred satin pumps, Daisy moved on.

The next nanny of interest was a small, thin woman called Nanny Venom. She was sipping tea with lemon, no sugar. There was look of acute disgust on her face. "My mummy and daddy are the Borbonskis," she said. "From Europe."

"The jewelry Borbonskis?" said Daisy, who had been doing her homework.

Nanny Venom's tiny mouth just about disappeared. "The jewelry Borbonskis are not in the Blue Book," she said, sniffing. "My mummy and daddy are the property Borbonskis."

"Got a lot of it, have they?" said Daisy casually.

"I should rather think they have," said Nanny Venom. "Nothing but nothing happens in the Neverglade property world unless they are involved. No land is sold, no building built without Mr. Borbonski's people hearing about it and sending the information back to him within the hour." She sniffed. "Next to Mr. Borbonski, Wayne Drayne is the merest minnow."

"Wayne Drayne?"

"An estate agent, what they call over here a real-estate guy. And a, ah, *country-and-western* singer. Whatever that is." Nanny Venom looked as if she knew perfectly well. "The Drayne so-called child is over there, naughty little sausage." She jerked her red nose at an infant dressed in a suit of fringed buckskins milling round a set of musical chairs. Daisy smiled sweetly, noting a slightly ginny whiff on Nanny Venom's breath, and passed a note to Nanny Pete. As usual, a plan was forming in her mind.

After Musical Chairs it was time for tea, and there was Primrose in bowler hat and apron, hardly visible behind a table groaning with good things. Nanny Pete seemed temporarily to have vanished, and so did Nanny Venom.

The birthday cake came in, blazing with candles, on a silver trolley pulled by sweet black Nubian goats. The children oohed and aahed. Little Otto Blaa de Klaa stooped to blow out his candles.

There was a sudden din of breaking glass and shouting. A gin bottle arched into the light and thudded into the cake. After the gin bottle came a wiry figure, dancing what looked as if it was meant to be a sailor's hornpipe. "Curse you all!"

it cried. "Your parents are monsters with more money than sense! Rule Britannia!" The figure then fell flat on its face and began to snore. It was Nanny Venom, and it reeked of gin.

"Well, well," said Nanny Pete, who had arrived to stand by Daisy. "Who'd a thought it, eh?"

"Thought what?"

"I give her a little shocking, like you suggested."

"Shocking?"

"Shocking pink, drink."

"Ah. Looks like more than one."

"Eighteen. Anyway, she told me she'd been in the navy," said Pete. "Dismissed for singing 'What Shall We Do with the Drunken Sailor,' the rude version, during an inspection by Her Majesty. After which there was no option but to go straight into the child-care industry, of course."

"Of course," said Daisy. "Well, I fear she will have lost her job." She clicked her tongue. "Now, children! Eat up, and then it is time for a treasure hunt!"

"With real treasure!" said Nanny Pete.

At six o'clock sharp, the enormous black Borbonski car drifted to a halt in the driveway. The chauffeur opened the door, bowing.

An endless brown leg in a blue shoe landed on the gravel. Mrs. Borbonski was fatter than the Baroness Blaa de Klaa, but not much. She slid into the Blaa de Klaas' world like a serpent entering a crystal vivarium. She looked languidly about her, raising one perfect eyebrow.

"Darlings, *darlings*!" she cried to a couple of children to whom she was not related.

"Ahem," said Daisy. "Over here, madam. Nanny Daisy at your service."

Mrs. Borbonski turned. Now that she came to look at the pair of children flinching alongside this tiny but respectful nanny, she realized that she had definitely seen them somewhere before. Hers! she now remembered.

"And *what*," she said, wrinkling her perfect nose, "is *that*?"

Next to small, brisk Nanny Daisy a plank was leaning against a pillar. Lashed to the plank was a grim, wiry woman smelling of gin.

"I wash led astray!" cried the wiry woman. "Tempted. You capitalish shwine. "OOOOOOoooooo, *wot* sll we do widda drunken sailah? *Wot* sll—"

"Who *is* that?" said Mrs. Borbonski, looking faint.

"Nanny Venom, madam," said Daisy. "She looks after your children."

"Oh, my *gaahd*," said Mrs. Borbonski. "Somebody tell her she's fired. But what am I going to *do*?"

Things were going exactly as planned. Daisy said, "As luck would have it, I am by happy chance available myself on a short-term contract. Sign here? Thank you."

If Daisy had not moved quickly, Mrs. Borbonski would

have hugged her. Leaving Pete and Primrose in charge of the Blaa de Klaas, off they purred to Skyrise Tower, whose gigantic penthouse was the principal residence of Albert B. Borbonski the Real Estate King.

The lift stopped at the ninety-third floor. The twins scuttled out and into a door marked NIGHT NURSERY. When Daisy went in, she found her charges standing rigidly to attention by their beds.

"Goodness me!" she cried.

"Don't torture us!" cried the little ones, whose names seemed to be Harry and Larry.

"Of course I won't," said Daisy. "Why should I?"

"Dumb Insolence," said Harry, in a robot voice.

"Wrong Attitude," said Larry, like a machine.

"We are sorry," said Harry.

"Very, very sorry," said Larry.

Both of them began to sob.

Daisy scowled. Goodness knew what cruelty Nanny Venom had used to produce this disaster. "Cocoa, anyone?" she said brightly.

Silence, with trembling lips.

"You were about to say, 'What's cocoa?' but you thought you might get into trouble," said Daisy. "Dearie, dearie me."

She made cocoa from a supply cupboard crammed with gin and chocolate that was labeled NANNY ONLY—TOUCH AND

DIE. The tinies slurped gratefully at the delicious bedtime beverage. "Now," said Daisy, "I'll read you a story. Where do you keep the books?"

"Books?"

"No books, eh?" said Daisy. "Well, I'll tell you a story."

She was exceptionally cross with Nanny Venom. For a moment she hovered on the brink of cheering herself up by telling them the awful tale of the Nanny Broken on the Wheel or the Nanny Ripped Asunder by Werewolves. But the twins were not ready. So she told them the story of Goldilocks and the Three Bears, leaving out the frightening bits. The boys went to sleep lying to attention under the covers, but with smiles on their anxious little faces. Daisy tiptoed out of the room.

She let herself out of the nursery and padded down an enormous staircase that looked out over the private dock and highly desirable yacht. Well, ship, actually. Nearly as big as the *Kleptomanic*.

Just what they were looking for.

Daisy went to the telephone and dialed.

Cassian was working in the Skeleton Cay generator plant when Daisy called him on his two-way radio. He listened, then said, "How many funnels?"

"Two."

"Size?"

"Several thousand tons."

"Excellent." He rang off. "Sounds like a ship for us," he said to the chief, who was helping his teddy bear regrind an outlet valve on the workbench.

"Schplendid," said the chief. His uniform was filthy and, ever since he had moved to his palace up the mountain, he smelled strongly of sulfur and rotten fish. "Edvard is not feelink normal without a ship. Nor me, nor me. Vill be excellent. *Nicht wahr*, Edvard?"

"*Heppy Christmas and a velcom to all*," said the voice of the Royal Edward, in a voice that had been modeled on that of the great Russian bass Chaliapin. "*Yes, please. Gute Nacht.*"

"See how delighted he is, mein Edvard?" said the chief, waggling the antique bed animal. "So sveet, so nice smellink—"

"So that's settled," said Cassian, cutting off the loony's flow. "We'd better go and have a look."

At the bottom of the Borbonskis' stairs was a vast hall. Here Daisy ran into a man in a tailcoat and muttonchop sideburns.

"Evening, Butler," said Daisy.

"Evening, Nanny," said the butler.

"Guv'nor in?"

The butler indicated a door with a white-gloved hand.

Daisy heaved open the enormous door and found herself

in an enormous room with enormous pictures of enormous naked ladies on the wall. It quite took her back to the Darling family home at Número Uno, Avenue Marshal Posh, now reduced to rubble. Half a football field away, at the far end of the room, was a crowd of enormous people, talking in low voices and jingling ice cubes in glasses.

A man was coming toward her, a thin man in a white suit. The room was full of overlapping pools of light. Somehow this man made his way between them so he was always in the shadows. Daisy started toward him. It was like walking in mud. She told herself not to be silly.

It was no good. The fact was that she was frightened.

She came to a halt. The man passed within six meters of her. As he passed, he turned his head toward her. He had shiny black hair, an eyebrow mustache, and dark glasses. He was Gomez Elegante.

Daisy took a step toward him. She meant to say, "Have you seen Mr. Colin Darling?" What she actually said was, "?"

The dark glasses turned for a moment in her direction. But Daisy was only a very small nanny in a brown bowler hat, not worth noticing. The dark glasses moved away. Daisy felt a small whirl of chilly air as he passed, and smelled a curious smell of patchouli and gardenia. And Gomez Elegante was gone.

Now that the chill had passed, she was hot and bothered, and her knees had a tendency to shake, and she was extremely cross with herself. She took a deep breath and told herself to remember she was a Darling with advanced nanny skills. She pulled herself together.

"Ahem," she said.

Nobody paid any attention.

"*A-hem,*" said Daisy, loud enough to crack the glass on a picture.

The people in the room jumped and turned. They found themselves looking down at a small, composed person dressed in a bowler hat, a green gingham shirtwaist uniform, and size-two brogues, one of which was tapping lightly but dangerously on the priceless Oriental rug.

"Who are you?" said Mrs. Borbonski, between perfect lips.

"I am Nanny Daisy," said Daisy. "You hired me earlier, remember? I have come to tell you that your children are in bed and it is time for you to come and kiss them good night."

"Them? Kiss? Good night?" said Mrs. Borbonski, flawless skin luminous with horror. "Do you know who I *am*?"

At that precise moment there was a rustle of silk suit, a jingle of ice cubes, and a luxurious creak of loafers. A huge figure sauntered out of the crowd. A voice mellow with Cuban cigar smoke said, "Step aside, love of my life. Well, little lady, so you are she?"

"Me is who?" said Daisy, frankly confused.

"The nanny of whom everyone in town is speaking."

The man was about two and a half meters tall and two and a half meters wide, smooth as armored glass.

Daisy felt flustered again. She heard herself say, "Er . . ."

"I am just back from a business trip to North Pork," said the huge smooth person. "When I come back from business trips, I always, that is to say sometimes, well, actually occasionally go say good night to the children. 'Scuse us, folks! Back in a jiffy!"

The very big guests made a delighted murmur. Any one of them would just as soon have kissed a rabid baboon as a child. But they admired the *idea* of fatherhood. And Daisy, trotting along to keep up with the man-mountain's steps, realized that this was a person who really loved to be admired.

Like someone else she knew. Someone called Papa Darling.

Outside the door, the big man started up the stairs. On the first landing, he turned and hung over her like an outbreak of bad weather.

"Don't ever do that again, honey," he said.

"I am not your honey."

"Everyone is my honey if I say they are, though you may always assume that I will definitely not be meaning it." The voice had become a snarl.

"So no good nights?"

Mr. Borbonski waggled his neckwear. "A million silkworms labored to make this tie in the sacred mulberry orchards of Tan Shan. You think I am going to risk a dwarf with a nervous stomach throwing up on it?"

"So you are a liar."

"Not about things that matter," said Mr. Borbonski.

Daisy did not often allow herself to think that grown-ups should be sent to bed without their suppers, but she found she was making an exception for Mr. Borbonski. She glanced at her watch. "You have not yet been out of the room for a convincing interval," she said. "So you have time to answer this question. Has a Mr. Colin Darling of Colossal Realty tried to sell you a place called Skeleton Cay?"

The eyes crinkled. They looked fierce and yellowish, not unlike the eyes of the Blaa de Klaas' Bengal tigers. Daisy dug her brogues into the stair carpet and made herself look right back. The fierce eyes slid away.

"What if he has?" said Mr. Borbonski.

"It is not his to sell."

"So he is a chiseler?"

"Or a low-rent schmuck," said Daisy fluently.

"Right," said Mr. Borbonski. "Now listen up, short person. Yes, a guy of this name did indeed offer me a hotel-and-fertilizer-works opportunity on some island or other, but I said, 'I deal in countries and bigger, so be off with you, and do not come back unless you can offer me Portugal or maybe Venezuela. Go see Wayne Drayne, who does the small deals,' I said. Now, nice as this has been, I have to—"

Daisy made a note in a small book with daisies painted on the cover. She said, "To the best of your knowledge, does Mr. Colin Darling have anything to do with Gomez Elegante?"

Mr. Borbonski's face went as white as Skeleton Cay beach sand, if not whiter. He said, "Who?"

"Gomez Ele—"

"Don't say that name."

"—gante, who has just left your house."

Mr. Borbonski said in a low, hoarse voice, "I do not know what you are talking about, but if I did, I would maybe suggest that you forget it right now and forget you ever forgot it and then forget that. Clear?"

"Not really," said Daisy truthfully. "I think you didn't buy the island off Colin Darling because you knew someone completely terrifying wants it and that person is Gomez Ele—"

"Noooo," moaned Mr. Borbonski. "That is to say, I can't remember and I don't want to. Ask someone else."

"Like who?" said Daisy, hot on the trail and reckless of grammar.

"Little people. Stupid people. People who do not mind putting gas in the car when their clothes are on fire. Maybe Wayne Drayne . . . how would I know? Now, I guess you have work to do, and so do I." He creaked back to his guests.

In the palatial nanny flat, Daisy toted Nanny Venom's old gin bottles to the garbage chute, where she stood on tiptoe to shove them into the slot. Then she wrote a note about nasty people to Dean the Wild Boy. Then she rang for the secretary, arranged for its express delivery, and prepared herself for sweet repose.

Very early the next morning, as a red sun was clambering up the towers of Neverglade City, an elegant steam launch puffed up to the dock at the foot of Skyrise Tower and tied up alongside the *Big Deal*. A boy in cutoff jeans scuttled out of the boat and away into the city. Then two figures in impeccable white tunics went up the huge yacht's companion ladder. One of them was large, the other small. The large one seemed to have a teddy bear buttoned into the front of his tunic.

"Good mornink," said the large one. "Ve have come to . . . er . . ."

". . . make an inspection on behalf of Neverglade Coast Guard," said the small one. "Top to bottom. Pollution, safety at sea, doorknob shininess, that sort of thing."

Lars Chance, captain of the *Big Deal*, shook his head wearily. "Don't you guys have anything better to do?"

"Ya!" said the big man, getting excited. "I could now be in mein bunk in Little Iceland, cuddlink ze Royal Edvard, so sveet, smellink so—aargh."

"Can't be helped, Captain," said the smaller coast guard, rubbing the elbow he had just driven into the bigger coast guard's ribs. "Just doing our job."

"Yeah," said the captain. "Well, if you must. You have oil on your nose, did you know that?"

"Oh. Gosh," said the small coast guard, who was of course Cassian, rubbing at his nose with his sleeve. "Come, Chief."

"Aye, aye," said the big one, who was of course Chief Engineer Crown Prince Beowulf of Iceland (deposed).

And the two of them commenced a detailed inspection of the *Big Deal*. When they had finished, they looked at each other.

Cassian said, "What do you think, Chief?"

"Perfect," said the chief.

"Just what I was going to say."

At that exact moment, Daisy was giving Harry and Larry Borbonski their breakfast. Primrose had popped over specially to cook it. There were five kinds of cereal, two kinds of sausages, excellent bacon, the eggs of happy hens, and many kinds of toast slathered in honey from a range of bees. Harry and Larry at first looked as if they suspected it might bite them. But such was its deliciousness that after a very short while it was they who did the biting. Soon all that remained were a scattering of crumbs and a lingering echo of rude but entirely understandable burps in the nursery air.

Daisy got them cleaned up and took them down to the visitors' gallery in Mr. Borbonski's study. There was a meeting going on. The poor little dears rapidly became extremely bored, but Daisy made them sit still, applauding when instructed, until she had marked in her notebook with the daisies on the cover the locations of the wall safes. Pete would be so grateful.

They went back to the nursery for a delicious brunch of buns and cocoa. The children had already gained enough confidence to throw a bun, though not very far.

"And now," said Daisy, when she had swept up the crumbs, "we shall go shopping."

Harry and Larry did not look enthusiastic.

"You know," said Daisy. "Buying things?"

"Like books of sums," said Harry sadly.

"And scratchy underwear," said Larry gloomily.

"Bows and arrows," said Daisy.

"Bows?" said Harry.

"And arrows?" said Larry.

Daisy nodded.

"Yay!" cried the tinies, punching their little fists in the air in a manner that would have had Nanny Venom groping in her ditty bag for the cat-o'-nine-tails.

"And so," said Daisy, "we will go to your mummy and get some cash."

"Cash!" they cried merrily, with more air punching.

Down the stairs they trooped.

Mrs. Borbonski was lying in a chair with cucumber slices

on her eyes. A small girl was polishing her toes. "You'll have to wait for Conchita to finish my nails," she said.

"Impossible," said Daisy. "The children will become restless. Things may get broken. Priceless things. I cannot answer for the consequences."

"Oh, dear, how *annoying*! Why does one *have* children? Such a *bother*!" said Mrs. Borbonski.

Harry and Larry looked extremely gloomy, poor mites, but Conchita stuck out her tongue at the cucumber eye sockets, and Daisy winked at her and squeezed the children's hands, and they seemed to brighten a little.

"The money," said Daisy.

"Work, work, work!" Mrs. Borbonski sighed, pushing a cucumber slice aside with a grunt of effort. "Behind the Picasso. No, not that one, the one on the left. Do you see a dial?"

"I do."

"The combination is twenty-four, twenty-four, twenty-four. Easy to remember. My real age."

"Seventy-two?" said Daisy, twiddling.

"Twenty-*four*," said Mrs. Borbonski. "Idiot!"

"Yes, madam," said Daisy. The safe was full of money and jewels. "Anything you say, madam. How much should I take, madam?"

"Oh, a handful," said Mrs. Borbonski. "Any you don't use you can bring back or something."

"Yes, madam," said Daisy. "Very generous, madam."

"Nobody understands the feelings of a mother for her children," said Mrs. Borbonski, becoming suddenly emotional and sitting up in her chair with a jerk that sent the cucumber slices flying left and right. The first thing she saw was Harry and Larry, smiling anxiously. "Eek!" she cried.

"Madam?" said Daisy.

"Who are these hideous midgets and what are they doing here?"

Harry and Larry started looking sad again.

"Off we go, children!" said Daisy brightly.

"Have a lovely time!" cried little Conchita the Toenail Girl.

Mrs. Borbonski lay back, sighing. "Nobody ever thinks about *me*," she said. "Where were we?"

"The left foot," said Conchita.

"Shut up and work," said Mrs. Borbonski.

It was quite a shopping trip.

First, Daisy sent a note to Nanny Pete, saying she would be bringing the Borbonski children to tea. Then she packed a small suitcase of money, summoned the chauffeur, and instructed him to convey her and the children downtown to Human Darkmouse, the world's greatest department store, where Harry and Larry played happily with hunting bows and arrows. It did wonders for their confidence and only one assistant got slightly punctured. When the gift wrapping was finished, they set off for tea.

It was a happy reunion in the luxurious Blaa de Klaa residence. The children ate hugely of the delicious Celebration Cakes baked by Primrose and played nicely (Twister,

87

Cranium, and a quick blast of Racing Demon). Poisonous spiders and other unsuitable hobbies seemed completely forgotten. The nannies chatted in a corner.

Daisy handed over to Nanny Pete the details of the safe locations at Skyrise Tower. "And," she said, "we are on the trail of Papa Darling."

"Great," said Pete. He did not look any happier.

"He may be in danger," said Daisy.

The happy cries of the Twister players seemed far away. It was clear to all that Papa Darling being in danger was fine by Pete.

"Well," said Daisy brightly, "can't sit here chattering all day. I shall pop to the Caddy and get the bows out of the trunk so the children can play with them."

"'Spose," said Pete.

There was more silence, during which Pete shook his head from time to time.

"Of all the ocean liners full of burglars in all the world," said Primrose, "you had to walk into that one. Now I am going to do a bit of cooking."

She trotted down to the main kitchens, where she was merrily greeted by the Blaa de Klaa cooks, who knew a genius when they saw one. Pete needed an Encouragement Bun. She rolled up her sleeves, opened her ingredients case, and reached for a bottle of the best Gung Ho. A shadow crossed her vision. She looked up.

"Dean the Wild Boy!" she cried in tones of pure delight. "You must be *starving*!"

Dean gave her his massive grin. "I got a note from your sister," he said. "She said you wanted to talk about nasty people. I kinda snuck past security."

"Wait!" cried Primrose. She erupted into a blur of saucepans. "Three-cheese omelet with hot-bread Caesar salad and cocoa on the side," she said, handing him a plate two action-packed minutes later. "Where have you been?"

"Around," said Dean the Wild Boy.

"Dean the Wild Boy," said Primrose, "there are things you have not been telling me."

"Mouth full," said Dean the Wild Boy.

"When Gomez Ele—"

"Nooooo!"

"—gante, be brave, ransacked the professor's pad on Skull Mountain, he was looking for something. What was it?"

Silence.

"Spit it out. In a manner of speaking," she added hastily.

Dean the Wild Boy said, "I gotta go."

Primrose said, "So you don't trust me?"

Dean the Wild Boy said, "I do so. Kind of."

Primrose stuck her nose in the air. "Do not," she said.

"Do too," said Dean the Wild Boy. "Hey!"

For with one swift movement, Primrose had tied him to his chair. "Now," she said, "either you spill some beans or I force-feed you five Truth Cakes and you will tell me what I want to know and then you will spend the next month telling big tattooed strangers that their breath smells like elephant dung and that when you were a little boy, you had a pink hippo called Jeremy and that deep down inside you love him still. This would be embarrassing. Eh?"

"Sure would," said Dean the Wild Boy glumly. "How did you know about Jeremy?"

"I know you so well," said Primrose, blushing, for it had been no more than an inspired guess. "Now, tell all, starting with when the professor sold us the island."

"Okay," said Dean the Wild Boy, shrugging. "He sold it to you because otherwise G-g-g—"

"Gomez Elegante."

"—would have taken it away. He'd been hassling Grandpa for months. He was on his way to get it that afternoon. He wants something, he takes it." Dean the Wild Boy shuddered.

"I saw his boat," said Primrose. "Out of the kitchen window. The *Kleptomanic* must have frightened him off."

"He moves in the shadows," said Dean the Wild Boy darkly. "Alone, except for fifty small bodyguards in dark suits. And now Papa Darling has the bill of sale for the island. And either G-g-g—"

"Oh, for gosh sakes, call him Jeremy," said Primrose.

"Noooo!"

"Dean the Wild Boy! Get a grip!"

"Sorry. Either he has Papa Darling and the piece of paper or he will have them soon."

"Papa is not stupid," said Primrose. "Just a little big-headed most of the time. So he will have hidden the piece of paper somewhere cunningly. And eventually Gomez Elegante will give up."

"No way," said Dean the Wild Boy. "There's something else."

"Yes?"

"The treasure."

Primrose laid down the saucepan she was holding, in case she used it to bean Dean the Wild Boy, whom she liked very much. "What treasure?" she said.

"Deathboy Ingleby's treasure."

"Who?"

"Five million pieces of eight, plus jewels and regalia swiped from the Sacred City of Popocacacacacac. Worth billions."

"We used to have billions," said Primrose. "It's only money. So this is on the island, is it? Where?"

"Dunno," said Dean the Wild Boy. "And now we never will."

"Wha?"

"I just went to see Grandpa," said Dean the Wild Boy. "He told me. You know that bit of paper he wrote on to hand over the island?"

"The one Papa Darling has got?"

"That one. Well, it's got Grandpa's note on one side. And on the other . . ."

"Yep?"

"Deathboy Ingleby's treasure map. Think," said Dean the Wild Boy, "of all the winning lottery tickets in the world and you get the idea of what having this map means."

"So what do you think?"

"I think that if your papa is going round town with that piece of paper, he is going to be a very badly wanted type of guy."

"Well," said Primrose, "we'd just better hurry up and find him. Well done, dear Dean the Wild Boy. Another omelet?"

"Don't mind if I do," said Dean the Wild Boy.

The trunk of the Borbonskis' Cadillac was as big as most people's bedrooms. Daisy opened it and pulled out the gift-wrapped bows and arrows for the children. As she arranged her armful, a voice said, "Ahem."

Daisy blinked. "Is someone in there?" she said.

"Yes," said the voice. A small figure crept on hands and knees into the bright patch the sun made on the floor of the

Caddy's trunk. It was Conchita, the little toenail girl. "I can't stand no more nails," she said. "Please, you no send me back."

"Of course not," said Daisy, helping her down onto the gravel. "Although . . ."

"I can do very good the nails," said Conchita, whose cheeks were streaked with tears. "But Señora Borbonski go always, 'Do my nails,' and in the meedle is telephone or cocktail and all is smodge and she go, 'Start again.' And is like painting huge breedge, when you finish little toe of right foot is time immediately to start again with little feenger of left hand. No time to eat, sleep, see friends. So I sheen down drainpipe and get into—"

"Drainpipe?" said Daisy.

"Yes. Anyway, then off we go and I hide and here we—"

"Ninety floors?"

"Yes."

Daisy saw once again the world spread below the glass lift, the awful swoop of Skyrise Tower, the huge floodlit yacht small as a toy in the dark far below. She seemed to hear the wind moaning in buttresses and girders, feel a flimsy plastic drainpipe in her fingers. She found herself dizzy with mixed fear of heights and admiration.

"Gosh, Conchita," she said. "What a nanny you would make! Here." She took the bowler hat from her head and thrust it on Conchita's.

The big brown eyes gazed levelly from under the brim, completely sick of nails, ready for any brat or drainpipe.

"Welcome aboard," said Daisy. "Now. Target practice here. Then I think we are going to leave you in charge."

They went up to the enormous Blaa de Klaa playroom and handed out the bows and arrows. The children started to attack various teddy bears and ornamental waterfowl.

"The devil finds work for idle hands to do," said Daisy, beaming at little Larry's innocent glee as he nailed a stuffed monkey at extreme range.

"But who knows where it will end?" said Nanny Pete, still gloomy, for Dean the Wild Boy's arrival had caused Primrose to forget all about the Encouragement Bun.

"Chin up!" said Daisy. "The closer we get to Papa, the closer we get to you taking off that dress and getting your striped jersey on again."

"Ah, well," said Pete, brightening. "Every cloud 'as a silver lining, eh, Daise?"

"That's the spirit!" said Daisy, clapping him on the back and hurting her hand.

They left Conchita to assist Pete. The next day, they would all go to tea at the Draynes'.

The hunt (said Primrose as she dealt the cards for a game of five-card stud) was on.

• • •

Back at the Borbonskis, Daisy watched the arrows whiz from end to end of the sixty-meter nursery and smiled indulgently. The Borbonski art collection was full of holes, but Harry and Larry were making great strides in self-confidence.

At lunchtime, when the Borbonski parents were out, Pete nipped round and did the safes. At teatime, Daisy piled Pete, Conchita, and the children into the long limousine and said, "Mush," to the driver.

The car rolled out of the city and into a land of green lawns and large square houses.

"Criminy!" said Pete Fryer.

At the end of a street, a huge guitar stood half buried in the ground. Its tuning heads were thirty meters in the air. Its frets shone like gold in the evening sun. Above its sound hole, which seemed to do duty as a gate, a huge rhinestone letter w lay on its back.

"What's this, driver?" said Daisy primly.

"The Lazy W ranch," said the driver. "Home a' Wayne Drayne the Cowboy Realtor. Like what you axed for."

The limousine plunged into the sound hole of the guitar and came to a halt in a dusty yard. Round the yard were log buildings: an enormous house, a long, low shed with a crudely painted sign that said BUNKROOM, and a tall building bearing the word SALOON.

"Hold it right there," said a voice. A small voice, with a

nasal whine in it, that came from inside a mop of dusty hair. A voice much smaller than the very large tomahawk in front of it.

"Hold what?" said Daisy.

"It," said the small person behind the tomahawk.

"What do you mean, 'it'?" said Daisy.

As far as it was possible to tell, the face under the dusty hair was frowning in a puzzled manner. "You're not supposed to ask that."

"And you're not supposed to wave tomahawks at people," said Daisy.

There was a pause in which a distant banjo played "Foggy Nervous Breakdown." The tomahawk wavered and dropped.

Pete Fryer stepped forward. "I'll take care of that," he said, twitching it from the tiny fingers.

Behind the dusty hair, the face seemed to be crumpling. "I want my mommy," said the whiny voice.

There was a flutter of bat-wing doors, a clatter of gold earrings, and the crunch of large cowboy boots in the dirt.

"Wayne Junior, you know your mommy is on tour right now," said a voice as deep as the Grand Canyon. "So you be a big guy and ask these little guys in and we'll see if we cain't rustle up a little something from the chuck wagon and maybe get ourselves a little real-estate action."

Reader, it would be easy to say that Daisy saw against

the tropical sun a man the size of a mountain. But reader, this would be wrong. Just about everybody in this story seems to be the size of a mountain. It is time for this to stop. The figure now looming above Daisy was two meters twenty tall in his Stetson hat. This is big for a person, but more the height of a hillock than a mountain, really. And it is not very exciting to say that one of the foremost country singers of Neverglade loomed over a small nanny like a hillock, is it?

Quite.

"I guess," said the voice, "you find me a mite scary, huh? Looming over you like a mountain an' all."

"Not really," said Daisy, for the reasons already explained. "Now then, tell me, who might you be?"

The hillock took off its hat and bent upon her a face that was used to being recognized and somewhat sulky that this did not seem to have happened. "Wayne Drayne, ma'am," said the voice. "Atcha service."

"Bless you," said Daisy, chin in air. She introduced her little group.

"Pleased ta meetcha," said Wayne Drayne. "Let's have ourselves a time."

"Tea first," said Daisy. "Then a time. Or the children will get hungry."

"Sure," said Wayne Drayne.

Daisy felt her nanny confidence waver as she realized that

this large show-off was in one way very like a mountain. His smile was warm and white, and his voice was warm and brown. But his eyes were cold and hard as rock.

"Well," he cried, "y'all git along into the saloon and grab some grits."

"Tea and buns would be most pleasant," said Daisy.

"Tea and buns is for dudes and pantywaists," said Wayne. "What you an' the kids gonna git in there is beans and beef jerky."

"How awful," said Daisy.

"Now, if you will excuse me, I have a meeting," said Wayne Drayne.

"Before you go—"

"Missin' you already," said Wayne.

He swaggered away across the yard. Four cowpokes fell into step behind him, their large hands on the butts of their large guns.

"Ahem," said a voice down by his knee. He looked down. The small nanny with the bowler hat was still there, marching alongside him with a pale but resolute look.

"Like I said," said Wayne Drayne, "I have a meeting."

"We'll come, too," said the nanny. "Pete?"

"Right there, Daisy," said the large nanny with the blue chin.

Wayne Drayne had heard that foreign nannies raised kids good. He was beginning to understand how they did it.

"In here?" said the one called Pete. "Good."

He opened a door. Beyond was a room with a guitar-shaped boardroom table and gold discs on the walls.

"In you go," said Nanny Daisy. "This won't take long." She turned a chair round, stood on the seat, and grasped the back with her small, firm hands. "Take your seats, please. Order."

Wayne Drayne and his henchmen found themselves sitting down.

"Now, then," said Daisy. "We want to talk about Skeleton Cay."

"Skeleton Cay?" said Wayne Drayne. "Never heard of it."

"Porky," said Pete, who was leaning by the door, blowing on his fingernails.

"Meaning porky pie, lie," said Daisy. "Pete is never wrong about that."

"Any road," said Pete, "Skeleton Cay."

"And Mr. Darling," said Daisy. "Mr. Colin Darling. Of Colossal Realty."

Wayne Drayne's craggy face turned sunset red. "Oh, *that* Mr. Darling," he said. "The Colossal Realty Mr. Darling. Why didn't you *say*?"

"We did," said Pete.

Wayne Drayne brushed him aside. "Mr. Colin Darling did indeed come to me and my associates," he said. "But I regret to say the synergies were not copacetic."

"What on earth does that mean?" said Daisy.

"He means they didn't like each other," said Pete, obviously warming to Mr. Drayne. "So what happened, Wayne?"

"He made me a proposition," said Wayne Drayne. "A good proposition. I was in agreement. He was goin' to get the certificate of ownership from someplace he had it hid. Then we were goin' to sign a paper, to make it all official. Then I was goin' to pay up. But then the hornswogglin' . . . That is to say, he got a better offer."

"Who from?"

Wayne Drayne began to bite his fingernails. "Do I got to tell you?" he said.

"You most certainly do."

"Don't wanna."

"I shall count to three. One—"

"Okay, okay!" cried Wayne Drayne. "You wanna know, this guy Darling gets a better offer from Gomez Elegante. So he says Gomez Elegante gets Skeleton Cay. And off he goes with Gomez Elegante."

"And where," said Daisy, "can I find Gomez Elegante?"

"You got any sense, you don't look for him."

"Why not?"

Wayne Drayne shuddered, making a noise like a maraca full of silver jewelry. "This Gomez Elegante, he is the kind of guy who comes to lunch, your lawn dies. Then he makes you an offer, and you better say yeah, because if you say nope, nobody sees you again, not ever. But even if you say yeah, he never pays."

"So he just takes things away," said Daisy.

"That is exactly what he does," said Wayne Drayne.

"Rude, naughty, and thievish," said Daisy.

"All them words was invented with him in mind," said Wayne Drayne.

Daisy said, "We need to know where Gomez Elegante lives."

"Li'l Miss Nanny, I neither know nor care," said Wayne Drayne in a low, passionate voice. "And you kin lock me up with a wagonload a' wildcats and you will get the same answer."

"I was thinking of locking you up with your son."

"There has to be a law against that," said Wayne Drayne, turning pale. "Some things in life is worse than gettin' ate alive." There was a long, agonized silence. Finally he said, "Okay, I give in. He comes and goes in planes. You could try the airport."

"We most certainly will," said Daisy, toes curling with triumph in her brogues. "Thank you for your time."

As they left, Wayne Drayne was shouting into a phone. "Get me the pilot!" he was yelling. "Get me out of here!"

Daisy and Nanny Pete walked back across the compound toward the saloon.

"The hunt continues," said Daisy, above the racket of the helicopter clattering into the yard.

"And who knows where it may lead?" said Pete.

Cassian and the chief were sitting on picnic chairs in an abandoned shed just down the wharf from Mr. Real Estate Borbonski's yacht, the *Big Deal*. It was the usual lovely Neverglade evening. Outside the shed, Skyrise Tower soared into the stars, twinkling with fairy lights at the top, for the Borbonskis were giving their usual dinner party. In the shed, Neverglade bats flitted among the rusty iron rafters, gobbling up Neverglade mosquitoes. Cassian was making a better mousetrap out of some wire he had found. Chief Engineer Crown Prince Beowulf of Iceland (deposed) was telling his teddy bear, Edward, about the *Big Deal*.

"Iss a pretty ship," he was saying. "You vill like it, Edvard, so good to sniffink you, so varm, so nice. I loff this ship, but no, you must not be jealous, because my heart belongs to you. Is roomy spacious and modern style, accommodation for two hundred peoples luxury class, up-to-the-minute kitchens, state-of-the-art spa units and all zis, but mit the prettiest diesel engines you every have seen. You vill loff them, Edvard, I know you vill. Only two can drive if needed—vell, three mit you, mein Edvard. And just now we go to steal this ship. Vot you say?" He pressed the bear's plush stomach with his thumb.

"Goot evenink, your royal highness," said the bear. "I vish you all ze good fortune in ze vorld. Aye, aye, good night."

"Argh," said Cassian, electrocuting himself slightly with the better mousetrap. A clock struck eight. "Time to go. Ready?"

"Und villink," said the chief.

Up from their picnic chairs they got. Out they went.

They had been watching the *Big Deal* for nearly a week, observing her routines. When she was in dock, her sailors went ashore every evening to carouse in the many grog houses of Neverglade, leaving only a couple of men on board. It should be child's play to overpower them and drive the ship away to the happy burglars of Skeleton Cay.

They walked round the corner of the warehouse. And there was the *Big Deal*, like a great white wedding cake in its floodlights.

"Gangplank ho," said Cassian.

They marched toward the gangplank. The Royal Edward was buttoned firmly into the chief's tunic. The chief told his bear what was going on in a low, regal Icelandic monotone.

At the foot of the gangplank, two men were standing. They wore dark suits.

"Who are you?" they said.

"Crew," said Cassian.

"Papers?" said the smaller man.

"Er . . ." said Cassian.

"Threat level orange," said the man into his radio.

In the shadows of the dockside buildings, people moved. They all had dark suits. They all seemed to be carrying . . . walking sticks?

Guns.

"Ah," said Cassian.

"Now is ugly little radio man to be crushed," said the chief to his bear. "Vait for it, *liebling*."

"Is this not the Fun Fun Fun floating Chinese restaurant and nightclub?" said Cassian.

"Ner," said the man.

"Silly me!" said Cassian.

"Now ist mein assistant rubbish talking," murmured the chief to his bear. "Now should we take out cutlass und *schtorm* der decks—"

"Sorry you were troubled," said Cassian.

With the speed of a cam valve realigning, he grabbed the bear from the chief and sprinted off down the dock. With a wail of grief and fury, the chief gave chase. The two white figures vanished into the dark in a thunder of sea boots.

"Threat level green," said the gangway guard. "Stand down, guys."

Round the corner, Cassian stopped and returned the bear to its owner.

"Here," he said. "Sorry."

"Mein!" cried the chief. "Mein, mein, mein, mein, *mein*

Edvard! Is all good viz you efter naughty man rip you avay, *liebling*? Is—"

"Ahem," said Cassian politely.

The chief stared. Nobody interrupted him when he was in conference with his bear.

"Two choices," said Cassian. "Forget the ship. Or make a plan."

"Forget? Make? Easy."

"So first," said Cassian, "into the *Polite Children*."

They climbed into the steam launch. Soon they were puffing eastward toward Skeleton Cay. The chief was talking to his bear. Cassian was thinking. Hard.

"Well," said Daisy, back at the Borbonskis'. "It seems our work here is done. Pete?"

"I got the contents of five safes. Jools, bit of silver and gold, portable antiques various, plus cash," said Pete, who was looking much brighter. "Captain said that should be enough."

"Of course she did. And the children, I think, are on the right road and have made suitable friends with whom they play nicely. All that remains is to find them another nanny."

"Ahem," said Conchita. "My family are poor but honest and I mus' take care of them. Daisy have taught me discipline and correct deportment. Primrose have taught me to make delicious food, plus I can do refried beans an' all that salsa that Harry like. And Larry already making good progresses in drainpipe sliding. They are nice keeds. I should like to stay, okay? And you, if you go see Gomez Elegante, be careful. Is bad man, smoggler, you know?"

"My dear Conchita," said Daisy, flashing her a winning smile, "I am sure there will be no problem at all."

And there was not.

Later that night, having handed over the reins of office (plentifully appliqué with sweet felt ponies), Daisy, Primrose, and Pete Fryer gave their brogues a final polish and headed for Neverglade Airfield.

There had been a briefing that morning at Camp Civility. The little inmates had been evacuated to the mainland the previous evening, each with a certificate of Good Behavior. Cassian had stood to attention in front of a group of selected burglars—the ablest-bodied and those who had taken most readily to life at sea. He had explained the plan.

"And the best thing about it," he said, "is that there is absolutely no dressing up as nannies."

There were disappointed noises from some surprisingly tough-looking burglars. But some of the rollers were delighted, particularly pretty little Sophie Nickit, who (if the truth be told) had been absolutely longing for a night out ashore wearing her own clothes and now saw her way clear to getting one.

When Cassian had finished, the captain took the stage.

"Comrades!" she cried. "This is your great opportunity. The hour is at hand for you to stand up for the great name of Burglar. Do not let it down!"

"Certainly not!" cried the burglars eagerly. "Hip-hip!"

"Hoorah!"

"Hip-hip!"

"Hoorah!"

"H—"

"All aboard!" cried Cassian, who had no time for displays of raw emotion.

Everyone ran out of the conference center and down the beach to the *Polite Children*. Two large able burglars pushed off. Looking round, Cassian noticed that someone was missing.

"Where's the chief?" he said.

"Search me," said the burglars.

"Wait," said Cassian. He jumped onto the beach and strode up the hill to Little Iceland.

The cod-drying racks smelled horrible. As Cassian pushed his way through the cloud of flies, he heard a great mechanical churning noise coming from the larger of the two huts. Mixed with the smell of cod was the smell of smoke. Cassian hammered on the door of the larger palace.

"Vot?" said the chief, sticking a rather sooty head out of the door.

"Time to go."

"Ach, I vill be forgettink mein own head next," said the

crown prince. He stumbled out of the door, accompanied by a cloud of smoke, and knocked on the door of the small palace next door. "Edvard!" cried the royal loony. "Is time for boat stealink!" He reached in, grasped the bear, and stuffed it into his tunic. "Restink," he said to Cassian. "Is needink much rest in zis hotness."

"Ah," said Cassian. "Off we go, then. Phew, that fish does stink. Is it rotten?"

"Is codfish, dryink to perfection Iceland style," roared the chief, eyes whirling with rage. "Vot I do not know about codfish and volcanoes can be written on grain of rice. Vun grain only."

"Ah," said Cassian. The fish looked pretty rotten to him. But what did he know about codfish? Or, for that matter, volcanoes?

Down the hill they went. And ten minutes later the *Polite Children*, deep-laden with burglars in shore-going trim, puffed away toward where the sun was setting over the towers of Neverglade City, leaving Dean the Wild Boy and a small band of unseamanlike burglars to look after Skeleton Cay.

There seemed to be a lot of big ships milling around in Neverglade Harbor. Ships full of diggers and dozers and dumpers.

"Just like the bad old dayf!" Nosy Clanger laughed.

"All gone now!" cried Sophie Nickit.

Reader, they spoke too soon.

But that comes later.

For now, the *Polite Children* slid over the horizon and the wisp of smoke from the right eye of Skull Mountain climbed the sky, where it joined another one, seeping from the smokestack of the larger of the two palaces in Little Iceland.

It was nice to have a night out from the *Big Deal*, thought Li'l FeeBee, the second mate. You had to wear your uniform, sure, and her taste was more for slinky Lycra leopard skin than a white uniform with gold braid. But Mr. Borbonski insisted on his crew being smart, and you got to cruise the waterfront, drink a little tea, and—with any luck—find someone to arm-wrestle. Though tonight was a slow night.

She sat on the terrace of the El Blotto Tea Room, nursing a cup of Earl Grey and watching the fireworks bursting from the mansion floors of Skyrise Tower, where the Borbonskis were having their usual dinner party. It was not a good evening. She was a second mate who liked company, and other people's fireworks always make you feel lonely.

"Mind if I join you?" said a voice at her elbow.

Li'l FeeBee looked up. There, smiling cheerily, was a woman exactly the same size as her, wearing exactly the kind of stretch leopard-skin sheath dress dear to Li'l FeeBee's heart.

"Be my guest," she said. "Do you by any chance like to arm-wrestle?"

"With or without a lit candle to burn the loser's hand?"

"Without."

"My favorite," said the little woman. "My name, by the way, is Sophie."

They arm-wrestled for a bit. Li'l FeeBee won, with just enough difficulty to make her extremely good-natured. Somehow, the conversation came round to clothes.

"I love your dress," said Li'l FeeBee. "It's so *me*."

"And I love your uniform," said Sophie Nickit (for it was she). "Why don't we swap?"

They went into the washrooms, giggling, and swapped. It did not occur to Li'l FeeBee to take her papers out of her uniform pocket.

"Won't be a minute," said Sophie. "See you back at the table?"

Li'l FeeBee sashayed back to the table, knowing everyone was watching her, feeling like a film star, not a boring old merchant seawoman. She sat down and wondered about ordering a pink cocktail. She would wait, she thought, until her new friend, Second Mate Sophie, came back.

Unfortunately for Li'l FeeBee, Sophie did not come back at all.

Deckie Malc waded through the bodies on the floor of the Dead Bad Fish Bar without noticing them. There was nothing odd about bodies on the floor at the Dead Bad Fish, except for the words tattooed on some of them, because dockside tattooists cannot spell. But bad spelling did not bother Deckie Malc, because to be bothered by spelling, you first have to be able to read, and Deckie Malc's education had ceased well short of reading.

He stopped, because his rock-hard belly had collided with the bar, and plunked two bunches of salami-sized fingers on the scarred Formica.

He said, "Usual, Toadface."

"Ur," said the tattooed plug-ugly behind the bar, reaching for a bottle of rum and a box of matches.

"I 'ates it," said Deckie Malc, because he did, even though he did not know what *it* was.

"'ates what?" said Toadface.

"It," said Deckie Malc. "All of it. Whatever *it* is."

"Me too," said Toadface, tipping out rum. He believed in

keeping his customers happy (which in Deckie Malc's case meant unhappy).

"Not many in," said Deckie Malc.

"Four conscious," said Toadface, striking a match. "Eighteen unconscious."

"I likes a fight," said Deckie Malc, accepting the pint mug of blazing rum and swigging hard.

"Hur, hur," said a voice beside him at the bar.

Deckie Malc turned. The man next to him at the bar was as big as him. Also, he seemed to have a handle sticking out of the back of his head.

"What you laughin' at?" said Deckie Malc.

"Hur, hur," said Giant Luggage (for it was he).

Deckie Malc clenched a boulder-like fist and took a swing. When the fist was halfway to target, something that felt like an airliner but was actually part of Giant Luggage collided with his chin. The world went black.

"Oi!" said Toadface. "What you doin'?"

"Hur, hur," said Giant Luggage, who was of course going through Deckie Malc's pockets, looking for his papers.

"In the Dead Bad Fish it is usual for the mugger to keep the paper money but for the barman to get the change. As a tip, like. And the barman is me."

Giant Luggage paid no heed. He straightened up and lumbered between the bodies to the door. The night swallowed him.

"Manners!" sniffed Toadface, relighting Deckie Malc's rum and draining the glass.

Nigel Spick, chief engineer, and Alan Span, second engineer, sat in a bright white restaurant. They had ordered spaghetti with white truffles and breast of chicken. Things that were not clean upset Nigel Spick and Alan Span. Only that day they had eaten their lunch off the top of the *Big Deal*'s number-two engine. It had been perfectly acceptable in hygiene terms.

Now, as they waited for their suppers to come, they were gazing at the flawless toe caps of their black shoes. Of course they had polished the shoes themselves. Which is to say they had first applied a thick layer of black cherry blossom, then melted it on with a red-hot spoon, then smoothed the polish with a fragment of whale's rib (blue, not fin, *never* fin). After that they had polished for ten minutes each with the hard, medium-hard, medium-soft, and soft brushes and finished off with three grades of duster. Time-consuming, certainly. But what they always said was that *if a job was worth doing, it was worth doing properly . . .*

Into the flawless toes of the shoes had swum the reflections of two faces. One was small and oily and needed a haircut. The other was large and pear-shaped and obviously loony.

"Ahem," said the oily one behind his hair.

Nigel Spick and Alan Span raised their eyes.

"Evenink," said the loony one. His white tunic was grubby, the two rows of medals on its left breast tarnished. Looking away from this awful sight, Alan Span noticed that his fork was point seventy-five millimeters out of alignment. Whipping a micrometer from his pocket, he checked, rechecked, and straightened up the offending cutlery.

"Nice evening," said the oily one—the *very* oily one, with an adjustable wrench tucked behind the left ear. The *none-too-clean* left ear, noted Nigel Spick. And if there had to be a wrench there, it should never be an adjustable, for adjustables knocked the corners off nuts. It should be a socket wrench. Well, a socket *set*, metric and imperial, to provide for any nut-size possibility. But one ear with a socket set hanging from it would be out of balance. If the left had one, the right should have one, too. Onto the mental TV screen of Nigel Spick there came a picture of this small engineer with a large socket set dangling on either side of his head. The ears would never take the load. . . .

Nigel Spick's head began to spin with a slow, sickening rotation.

"Und," said the one with the pear-shaped head, "also is the Royal Edvard sayink good evenink." He burrowed inside his filthy tunic and pulled out what seemed to be a teddy bear. "Good evenink!" cried the loony, clapping the bear's hands. "You can kiss him. Kiss him!" And he thrust the bear into the pale, beautifully washed faces of Engineers Spick and Span.

They found themselves staring at a bear's nose, stained with drool, smelling of old bedclothes and engine oil, on which someone had written in felt-tip pen *I lof him I lof him I lof him*. It was the worst thing they had ever seen or smelled or, as it turned out, tasted. The world spun round one more time, darkened, shrank, and went out.

"Well," said Cassian, crouching by the unconscious engineers and going through their pockets. "That was easier than I thought it would be."

Cabin Boy Hawk "Shorty" Dork liked coming ashore. A very small busybody who was a lot older than he looked, he loved to skateboard. On the *Big Deal*, skateboarding was greatly discouraged. Mr. Borbonski might be a trillion-aire, but he knew what wore carpets out. So Cabin Boy Hawk Dork spent his nights ashore, zooming round his favorite underground parking lot, letting off a bit of steam.

As he rumbled down the *Big Deal*'s gangplank and followed the arrows for the PARKING signs, he became aware that someone was sprinting alongside him. When he looked round, he saw a very small person standing on a plank. To the bottom of the plank someone seemed to have screwed a pair of roller skates. Pathetic apology for a skateboard, thought Shorty.

"Rafe you!" said the small person, who was heavily tattooed, entirely toothless, and standing on one leg.

"Awright!" screamed Shorty, making what he imagined were Hawaiian surfing gestures at Nosy Clanger (for it was he).

Reader, I will not attempt to describe the catalog of phat maneuvers upon which these tiny people now embarked. Suffice it to say that no part of that very large multistory parking lot was unmarked by their wheels. Including the ceilings.

"Right!" roared Nosy when, after an hour, they found themselves on the topmost level. "Laft one to bafememp lebbel 'f a rubber duck!"

He started off down the spiral ramp.

Reader, it has rightly been said that while a person just under two meters high may be a bit competitive, a person well under one meter high will be a bit more competitive. Shorty was exceptionally keen to catch up.

"Follow my leader!" cried Nosy pluckily. "Bet you can't!"

"Bet I—whoa," said Shorty, smoke pouring from his wheels as he drifted round the right-hand curve of the ramp to Level 3.

But Shorty was a geek. He had hand-installed racing slicks and high-temperature bearings and slathered Kazakhstan beeswax stick-fast lotion onto the board rails. Reader, Nosy Clanger went like a bat out of hell. But Hawk

"Shorty" Dork went like a matched pair of bats out of a lower hell, and the bats were state of the art, bred for speed and road-holding.

Where were we?

Ah, yes.

The two tiny skaters zoomed off the ramp into the basement, neck and neck. Ahead of them was parked a Lamborari Superleggera, the world's most beautiful sports car, a long, low wall of gleaming scarlet perfection.

"Under!" shrieked Clanger.

"Over!" shrieked Shorty.

"Chicken!" shrieked Clanger.

"Am not!" screamed Shorty, the slipstream pulling his face out of shape.

They thundered down on the Lamborari.

Reader, you may be a champion skateboarder, and you may be exceptionally small. But a Lamborari's ground clearance is seven-point-six centimeters. Nobody, *nobody* can skateboard under a Lamborari, and only a total moron would even try.

Hawk "Shorty" Dork was exactly that kind of moron. Trusting to fate, he went under.

Fate let him down.

There was a crash of breaking glass, plastic, skateboard, and teeth.

"Hoppla!" cried Nosy Clanger, leaping effortlessly over

the sports car and stopping with a Split Banana and a cloud of burning rubber. "Oopsh."

Shorty's head seemed to be embedded in the driver's seat of the sports car. His feet stuck out of the passenger's window.

Grunting, Nosy pulled him out. He appeared to be sleeping peacefully. Executing a small New Zealand *haka* dance of triumph, Nosey found Shorty's papers, pocketed them, and scooted away into the night. Behind him, the Lamborari's burglar alarm emitted an electric caterwauling. Police sirens wailed in the distance.

Shorty would be well looked after.

The crew that walked up the gangplank of the *Big Deal* that evening were roughly the same size and shape as the crew that had left on shore leave, but they were by no means the same people. The *Big Deal*'s genuine crew were mugged, rolled, trussed up, sleeping, or just waiting for new friends who had popped out for a second and would never come back. The men and women who showed their papers to the bored security guards were burglars in disguise, no more, no less.

"Now, then," said Cassian. "Are we ready?"

Captain Lars Chance was sleeping peacefully in his cabin. He had sailed the world's oceans, working his way up the ladder of ships from cabin cruiser to merchantman, merchantman to ocean liner, until he had reached the summit of his career: captain of the *Big Deal*, the world's biggest, most advanced, most luxurious private yacht. These days, Captain Chance did not bother to go ashore. The *Big Deal* was his world and he was happy in it.

Now, as his eyes flicked open, he was instantly aware that something was not right. The ship's engines had started. There were voices in the wheelhouse just outside his cabin.

"Cor," one of them said. "Wonder what that's for?"

There was the sound of a switch clicking.

"Floodlights," said another voice. "Amazing. Try that one."

Another click. A sort of roaring hiss from the funnel.

"Whoa," said the voice. "Who put the lights out?"

Captain Chance knew exactly what had happened. These meddling fools had turned on the anti-paparazzi smoke generator. Dense black fumes would be billowing from the funnel, covering Neverglade with a dark and impenetrable fog. He sprang from his bunk and rushed into the wheelhouse.

Two large men were standing at the bank of switches. Beyond the bridge windows, the world had turned oily black.

"Who are you?" said the bigger man.

"I am the captain!" cried Lars, heading for the alarm button.

"Wrong!" said a woman's voice.

Lars turned and found himself facing a tall, dark woman—a vision of svelte elegance in an exquisitely tailored white uniform decorated with captain's gold braid of a depth and richness that matched her voice.

"How did you get on board?" he said, blushing violently, for he was dressed only in none-too-clean boxer shorts and a torn sleeveless undershirt.

"I walked. I had ordered my uniform from the local branch of Balenciaga. Rather divine, do you not think?"

"Fabulous," said Captain Chance, ready to swoon. "That is to say, they should never have let you up the gangway."

"People normally do," said the captain. Her dark eyes traveled from his toes to his head. One of her eyebrows rose a fraction of a millimeter.

All parts of Lars Chance began blushing at once. He bolted back into his cabin. Pulling on his uniform, he bellowed, "You won't get away with this!"

"Actually I rather think we probably *will*," said the golden voice of the captain. "And you will help us."

"Help you?" barked Lars. "Never!"

"In that case, we will just have to manage by ourselves," said the captain. "But I fear we may break your lovely ship."

"Nooooo!" cried Lars.

"The choice is yours," said the captain. "Lock him in that cabin." The lock clicked. "Engines started, I believe. Let go fore and aft? Good."

"But we can't see," said a voice.

"We'll risk it," said the captain. "Who cares about a dent or two?"

Lars came to a decision. Never mind who was in control of his beautiful ship. The important thing was that she did not get bent or sunk. "I will cooperate," he said. "Turn on the radar and let me out of here, and I will do as you ask."

"Marvelous," said the captain.

And Lars found he was feeling warm and happy all over.

Back on Skeleton Cay, Dean the Wild Boy sat in the top of a palm tree and dropped nuts moodily onto the beach far below. Since the ship-nicking expedition had left, the only sounds on Skeleton Cay were the wind in the trees, the surf on the reef, and the odd snore of a dozing burglar.

Once, Dean the Wild Boy could have been happy with these sounds. Now the island seemed too quiet. He missed the distant skirl of a burglar's hornpipe, the clatter of Primrose's saucepans on the range. Particularly the saucepans.

Tossing a final coconut to the ground, Dean the Wild Boy shinnied down the tree and set off across the old familiar island. They had left him to look after things and look after things he would. Well, not so much look *after* as look *for*. As in look for treasure.

He quartered the undergrowth, searching for the hundredth time for the glint of gold, the splinters of a chest, a bone pointing in a direction. But undergrowth grows quickly in the tropics. There was no gold, no bones, no splinters. Without an X to mark the spot, it was hopeless. The only sound was the wind in the trees. And come to think of it, a strange buzzing . . .

Dean the Wild Boy raised his eyes from the ground. He saw that his wanderings had brought him close to the palaces the chief engineer had built on the hillside. The humming was actually the buzz of flies attracted to the cod rotting on the washing lines outside the palace. A chance puff of breeze wafted the smell to Dean the Wild Boy's nostrils.

"Argh," he said, backing swiftly away.

Later, he wandered up Skull Mountain and watched the horizon. It was empty. But sooner or later, G-G-*Gomez Elegante* would come. The name made him shiver. Then he realized that he was shivering from habit, not from fear.

"Gomez," he said aloud.

He checked himself for shivers, found none.

"Go. Mez. El. Egg. Ann. Tay."

Still no shiver. A name was all it was. Thank you, Darling children, and particularly Primrose, he thought. You have shown me that the only thing to fear is fear itself. In fact, if Gomez Elegante was going to come up against the Darling children, it was almost possible to feel sorry for the guy. . . .

Wait a minute, thought Dean the Wild Boy. This is not

Jeremy the bedtime hippo we are talking about here. This is Gomez Elegante and I am being seriously overconfident.

Suddenly the horizon to the west was covered in ships.

The shivering came back. But Dean the Wild Boy did not run away. He summoned what burglars remained, spat on his hands, and started to rebuild the Home Landslide.

The name badge on the woman at the information desk of Neverglade Airfield said she was called Lulubella Nice. Primrose thought she looked more as if she should have been called Lotta Rage. Her eyes were hard and blue, her smile steely. A half-drunk cup of coffee stood at her elbow.

"Mr. Gomez Elegante?" she was saying. "Never heard of him."

"He keeps his airplane here," said Daisy patiently. "And if you do not know him, perhaps you could introduce us to someone who does?"

Lulubella could not remember ever finding herself talking to small, obstinate nannies with bowler hats pulled down over their noses accompanied by larger nannies definitely in need of a shave before. But that was the fun of airport work: it gave you the chance to say "no" to so many different kinds of people.

"No," she said.

Daisy sighed. "In that case," she said, "I am sorry you were troubled, and we will ask you when you feel better."

"I feel fine, thank you so *much*," said Lulubella with secret glee. She loved it when people gritted their teeth.

The nanny was saying something.

"Poddin?" said Lulubella.

"What does the notice board say?" said Daisy, pointing.

Lulubella's eyes swiveled to the notice board. "Can't you *read*?" she said scornfully.

"Oh," said Daisy. "Yes. Actually. I just remembered. I can."

"Well, then," said Lulubella, draining her coffee.

It tasted odd; rather delicious, actually. That was because when Daisy had been directing her attention to the notice board, Primrose had tossed a couple of her Do Right Drops into the cup.

"Next!" said Lulubella.

"Ahem," said Daisy, in a voice like a whip cracking.

Lulubella blinked. The bowler hats went in and out of focus. Between them, the little nanny with yellow hair gave her a soupy . . . no, a *sweet* smile. She longed to know these lovely people better. But how? Ah, yes. She would do absolutely anything they wanted. Anything to stop the bigger of the small nannies scowling like that and using that awful voice. Lulubella found that her tongue was hanging out, and that she was panting, and that she wished she had a tail so she could wag it.

"Now, then," said Daisy. "Please show us to the plane of Gomez Elegante."

"Yes, of *course*," said Lulubella. "And it is not plane but planes. They live in the secret hangar. Nobody knows about it except a few of the staff. Mr. Dixon told me about it so I would not tell anybody else. He's the airport manager. He likes me. He wants me to have dinner with him and maybe have his babies, but he can go—"

"That's enough of that, thank you very much," said Daisy. "Take us to this secret hangar. And afterward, you can wash your mouth out with soap and water and forget you ever saw us."

"Oh, goodie!" cried Lulubella, and trip-trapped off on her high heels, with Nanny Primrose, Nanny Daisy, and Nanny Pete close behind.

Through the luggage department they marched. On the tarmac, they turned toward the long, low sheds where the airplanes were kept. They walked through the doors of Hangar 2, under the wings of the parked planes, straight toward the back wall, where a radio stood on a workbench. Lulubella turned on the radio and twisted the tuning dial. Salsa music blared into the hangar. A section of the wall slid back.

"Neat, huh?" said Lulubella.

There in the secret hangar were half a dozen twin-engined airplanes, all painted dark blue with gold piping, with the initials GE intertwined on the tail fins.

From an inner pocket, Daisy whipped out a picture of Papa Darling. "Have you seen this man?" she said.

Lulubella's face crumpled. She began to whimper.

"She can't tell us," said Primrose. "It's the drops. She can only do what she's told. If she can't do it, she just gets into a state, that's all."

"Oh, all right. Run along, then," said Daisy. "Back to work. Close the door behind you. And don't forget the soap and water."

"Great!" trilled Lulubella, smiling a great blond smile. "Byeeee!" She fluttered her fingers and trip-trapped away toward the washrooms.

Pete shook his head. "Old man," he said.

"Old man?"

"Old man's beard, weird."

"Ah. What," said Daisy to Primrose, "do you *put* in those drops?"

"Essence of Faithful Hound as usual. Scopolamine. Rainwater from the gutters of the Temple of the Good Servant. Sugar, rose water, all that sort of stuff."

"Ahem," said Pete. "'Scuse me, but are we going to stand

round nattering all day, or are we going to have a look in these arteries?"

"Arteries?"

"Arteries and veins, planes."

"Ah. Yes, of course. Let us take one each."

The airplanes were less glossy inside than out. They had four seats at the front, partitioned off from a large cargo hold at the back. They were clean and tidy and contained absolutely no clues. The searchers met on the hangar floor.

"Anything there?" said Daisy.

"Nothing," said Primrose.

"Nick," said Pete.

"Nick?"

"Nick and filch, zilch."

"Ah," said Daisy.

"Except," said Pete, "mine does pen and ink."

"Pen and ink, stink," said Primrose, ever helpful.

"I did actually understand," said Daisy. "What of?"

"Diesel," said Pete. "Plus scent."

Daisy frowned. Somewhere at the back of her cathedral-sized mind, a bell was ringing.

"Let's have a Dover," said Primrose.

"Dover?" said Pete.

"Dover cliff, sniff."

"The next person who uses made-up rhyming slang," said Daisy, "will have me to deal with."

"Return of the," said Pete.

"Return of the?"

"Return of the Jedi, ready," said Primrose.

"Steady. Ow," said Pete, clutching his foot, on which Daisy had precision-stamped with her size-two brogue. "Sorry."

"Granted," said Daisy, and marched toward the plane.

"Up in the cockpit," said Pete.

They trooped into the cockpit and sniffed deeply.

Primrose frowned, her sensitive cook's nostrils flaring to catch every molecule. "Patchouli. And jasmine. No, gardenia. And of course diesel. Where, oh, where, have I smelled this before?"

"I know," said Pete, in a voice oddly surly. "It was on the letter what your papa sent to the captain."

"And it was on Gomez Elegante at the Borbonskis'," said Daisy. "We are getting warmer." She shivered.

"Maybe," said Pete.

Daisy put a hand on his arm. "Chin up," she said, for she knew Pete loved the captain and saw Papa as his rival for her affections. "He has really gone and done it this time, and she will not forgive him."

"You think so?" said Pete, brightening.

"Who can speak of the workings of the human heart in all its twisted wonder?" said Daisy, who had read it somewhere.

"We reckon it is about two to one she fancies you more than the old man," said Primrose, less poetically. "Oi! What's that?"

Voices were talking in the hangar. The door rumbled open. Cuban-heeled footsteps clattered across the concrete floor.

"They're coming this way!" said Daisy.

"There's no back door!" said Primrose.

"Quick! In the bog!" said Pete.

"What if one of them . . ."

"Fingers crossed," said Pete, hustling everyone into the tiny lavatory and locking the door.

There was the sound of people clambering into the plane.

"With any luck, they've just popped in to check something. . . ."

The rest of his consoling remarks were drowned by the roar of the engines starting up.

"Wha?" shouted Daisy.

". . . or then again, maybe not," said Pete.

The floor trembled underfoot. The airplane started to move.

"What now?" mouthed Daisy in the din.

"Wait and see," Pete mouthed back.

The sound of the engines rose to a buzzing roar. The airplane accelerated out of the hangar, bounced down a runway, and became airborne. Outside the little porthole of the lavatory the towers of Neverglade sank into their haze. The engine note faded as the plane throttled back and settled to its flight path.

"Up, up, and away," said Primrose.

"Stand back," said Nanny Pete, removing his bowler hat and wig and mopping the eagle tattoo on his head with a red-spotted hanky. Very gently, he pulled back the bolt and opened the door.

The cockpit door was shut. The cargo door was open. Beside it stood a stocky man in a dark suit, peering out at the ground.

"Boomps-a-daisy," said Pete, stunning the fellow with a blow of his bowler hat. He stripped off the man's suit, donned it, and dressed the man in nanny gear. Then he strapped a parachute to the man's back and heaved him out of the door.

"A

    a

        a," said the man, plummeting.

Pete stuck his head out of the door. "Landed in a sewage farm," he said when he pulled it back in. "Nasty, but perhaps he'll get out swim. Swim and dive, alive. Sorry," he said hastily, seeing Daisy's face.

"Ah," said Daisy.

"And in the suit pockets," said Pete, rummaging, "we have a family-sized skinning knife. It occurs to me that these are nasty, dangerous people."

"All the more reason for saving Papa," said Daisy stoutly.

"Yerse," said Pete, a lot less stoutly.

They watched out of the door as the city fell behind and the plane droned over the sea.

Primrose was picking idly with the skinning knife at a large bale lashed to the middle of the airplane floor.

"Wait!" said Pete.

"Hang on. Oooh . . ."

"Too late," said Pete.

Primrose had unpicked a corner of the bale. The cargo hold with its open door was a draughty place. The bale seemed to be full of paper. Bits of it rushed and fluttered round the cabin, drifted out of the door, and settled like a snowstorm on the tropical blue sea. There were ships down there: fifty or sixty of them, loaded with diggers and dumpers and dozers and piles of gravel and bags of cement, all beetling steadily southeastward, toward the dim hump of an island with smoke rising from its central bump. Toward, in fact, Skeleton Cay. As the first bits of paper landed among them, the ships slowed and stopped. Several of them bumped into each other. Tiny figures ran around on decks, launching lifeboats.

Daisy put her hand in the air and grabbed one of the slips of paper. "Hmmm," she said, holding it up to the light. "Just as I thought."

"Wha?" said Pete.

"Money."

Pete's jaw dropped. "All of it?"

"I expect so." Daisy did a sum in her head. "Fifty million dollars, maybe."

"Criminy," said Pete, dazed.

"So you'd better sit on the bale," said Primrose. "Before it all flies out of the door."

"But . . ." said Pete.

"Mr. Gomez Elegante smuggles stuff to Neverglade, like Conchita said," said Primrose. "In the airplane. And you can just about bet it is not tins of beans. Then people pay him for the stuff and he takes the money back to his place."

"Poor Papa!" said Daisy. "In the power of such a man!"

"It's fine," said Grimrose primly, or rather Primrose grimly. "The Darlings are on the case."

"You have to feel sorry for this Gomez," said Pete. "Now, let's stuff this here bale with them there life jackets, and get you hidden, and see what we shall see."

He shut the children in the overhead bins and sat on the bale. The ships fell behind, the smoke of collisions rising. Ahead, other islands came up over the horizon. The plane started to descend.

Working on Skull Mountain, Dean the Wild Boy saw the black plumes of smoke rise from the sea to the northwest. He saw a little silver speck drone across the sky. Soon after that he saw a white ship, beautiful as a wedding cake, glide from the direction of Neverglade, slide round the point, drop anchor in the lagoon, and send a boat to the beach. He rushed down to the landing place to greet it.

Onto the snow-white sand stepped the captain, Cassian, and several burglars. Lars Chance had been dropped off in a rowboat halfway to Neverglade. He had whimpered, but he would be fine.

"Well, my dears," said the captain to the excited throng of burglars that flocked around. "Out there in the lagoon you see our new ship. How do we like her?"

"Lovely," said Dean the Wild Boy.

"And we'll try not to run this one aground."

There was much hearty laughter.

Dean the Wild Boy reported his sighting of ships on the horizon. "To Skull Mountain for a better view!" he cried.

The captain kicked off her classic white kid casuals and put on a pair of stout but elegant walking boots. Off they set.

The view in the telescope was clear: a circle of blue in which milled a large selection of rusty old barges loaded with earthmoving machinery, materials for making concrete, and other building stuff.

"Sixty-two, sixty-*three*," said the captain, counting off ships on her scarlet-tipped fingers. "Dearie me." She passed the telescope to Cassian. "What do you think?"

Cassian watched and grunted. "Basically, they're coming this way."

"With diggers and dozers and dumpers, and enough stuff to build villas and hotels and probably a fertilizer works. Oh, dear me. Do we detect Papa Darling's hand in this?"

"Highly probable," said Cassian, scowling.

"Or Gomez Elegante," said Dean the Wild Boy.

"Gomez?" said Cassian.

"I'm not scared anymore," said Dean the Wild Boy.

"Maybe you should be," said Cassian.

"What shall we *do*?" said the captain.

"Leave it to me and Dean the Wild Boy," said Cassian.

"Bring 'em on," said Dean the Wild Boy.

Some distance to the south and west, the airplane of Gomez Elegante flopped out of the sky, bounced twice on the private runway of Gomez Elegante's private island, and came to a halt in a small, dirty cloud of burning rubber. The cockpit door opened. Three men in dark suits and darker glasses came out into the cargo hold.

"Vargas!" they cried, when they saw it was empty. "Vargas, where are you?"

No reply.

"Search the plane," said the one called El Teniente.

They looked in the loo. They looked in the bins. Finally they looked in the bale of money and found that most of the banknotes had been replaced by life jackets.

"Ah," said El Teniente. "He has stolen the moneys and made a jump for it."

"Stolen the moneys," said the other two men, who were one and a half meters tall and needed a shave. "Is not good."

"Is not good for Vargas," said El Teniente.

"Heh, heh, heh," said the unshaven men.

"*Vamonos,*" said El Teniente.

They marched off. Their coat pockets swung as if they contained heavy things: like, for instance, family-sized skinning knives. Just for instance.

Four hundred meters to the north and east, down the runway and a bit to one side, one shaved head with an eagle tattoo and two brown bowler hats with white tropical covers rose from the sun-dried scrub. They watched the little figures in dark suits strut into the heat shimmer.

"Ow," said Daisy.

"What?" said Primrose.

"Scraped my knee."

"Bruised my elbow," said Primrose.

"If you think you can jump out of a plane that has just landed without messin' yerself up a bit," said Pete, "you are livin' in a dream world."

"Well!" said Daisy, rising and dusting herself down.

"There is nothing wrong with dreams. Now, let us find somewhere for a wash and brushup."

"And some food if possible," said Primrose.

"Listen," said Nanny Pete. "These are bad people."

Daisy gave him a kind, patient smile. "Pete," she said, "if I've told you once, I've told you a thousand times. There is *nobody* as bad as us."

Pete opened his mouth.

"And none of your rhyming slang, thank you very much," said Daisy. "I seem to remember seeing a big house somewhere over this way."

She began to march down the runway.

Pepe Monstruo was dozing in the west gatehouse, his nostrils full of the soothing smell of the oil with which he had been anointing his skinning knife. There were sun, sand, sea, and the usual faces. It was the usual kind of day, except that the attack dogs all seemed suddenly to have gone to sleep and Gomez Chico had not shown up. Thank goodness. Pepe Monstruo had spent years in prison for robbery and murder. He had even spent a week at school, before he had been expelled for painting rude pictures on the wall of the teacher's house, having an artistic tantrum, and burning it to the ground. But he had never, ever in his grim, violent life met anything as awful as Gomez Chico, which is what people called Gomez Elegante Junior. There had been gunfire earlier on. Probably Gomez Chico playing with his pet rabbits.

"Good morning," said a voice.

Pepe Monstruo stood up. He was looking at two small people in gingham dresses and bowler hats and one larger person wearing a dark suit. Pepe Monstruo picked up his skinning knife.

"Put that nasty thing away," said the larger of the bowler hat people sternly. "You might take someone's eye out."

Pepe Monstruo was about to say that that was the general idea when he found he had indeed put the knife down. To cover up his confusion, he said, "Wha you wang?"

"We are two nannies and a sailor," said the larger bowler hat person. "We have unfortunately been shipwrecked and washed ashore. Naturally we have dried and ironed our clothes. Now we are in need of food and shelter."

"Wha is nangy?"

"We specialize in the care of children." Daisy noticed an odd expression trickle over Monstruo's gorilla-like features. She also noticed the ground was strewn with broken toys. "*Difficult* children," she said. "Are you all right?"

For Pepe Monstruo had dropped to his knees and was babbling thanksgivings. "*¡Sí, sí!*" he cried when he was once more capable of speech. "Oh, life so kind, so kind!"

"I beg your pardon?"

"Com this way," said Pepe Monstruo. "There is some mangs who weel be very please to see you."

"Do pray lead on," said Daisy.

The road to the house was made of crystal gravel, flanked with dark, cone-shaped cypress trees and littered with more broken toys.

"Tch," said Daisy, picking up a piece of torn metal and frowning. "The Slotbody and Pring Radio-Controlled Helicopter, fragment of fuselage."

"Year's wages, that costs," said Pete.

"The duty of the spoiled brat? To show its daddy where life's at," said Primrose.

They proceeded in grim silence to the house.

The house was not silent. There was a salsa band playing somewhere. In the marble front hall, half a dozen large ladies in small swimsuits were sitting round an ornamental fountain, chattering in Spanish.

The hall was even bigger than the one at Avenue Marshal Posh. A double staircase swept down from a gallery. From the room beyond the staircase came voices.

"The chief," said Monstruo. "I take you to heem. Come to the waiting room." He walked the forty-odd meters to a door that was ajar and pushed it open.

Something plummeted out of the sky. Suddenly Monstruo was not a dark-haired man in a dark suit, but white as a Druid in robes. He blundered to and fro, bumping into things, swearing horribly in a Spanish that bubbled. Daisy and her companions frowned.

"The old bucket-of-whitewash-on-the-door trick," said Primrose. "Out of the ark or what?"

"Certainly most old-fashioned," said Daisy. She strode up, stood on tiptoe, and rapped on the bucket with her knuckles. "Lie down!" she cried.

Monstruo kept on staggering in a circle. Daisy put out a brogue and tripped him. Down he went, crash, full length on the marble floor. Kind Daisy stooped and tugged the bucket from the man's head.

For a moment the face was a mask of whitewash. Then the black eyes flicked open, burning like hot bullets.

"¡Bastante!" he cried. "Enough! This Satan brat, balance the bocket, 'e drive me crazy! Either 'e go or I go!"

The air in the room turned suddenly chilly and smelled of patchouli.

"Ay, Monstruo," said a smooth, cold voice. "Then you go, I theenk. The crocodiles are lonely in their swamp. Take heem away so he can teach them how to play el water polo."

Daisy looked up. Leaning against the door frame was Gomez Elegante, stroking his narrow mustache. He was wearing a white suit. Behind him stood half a dozen men wearing black suits. Some of them dragged Monstruo away. The ladies in the small swimsuits had fallen silent and were bristling with goose pimples.

"And 'oo," said Gomez Elegante, "are you?"

"Shipwrecked nannies and one merchant seaman," said

Daisy, through teeth that badly wanted to chatter. "Monstruo was very kindly bringing us to see you. Not anymore, it seems."

Gomez Elegante had eyes that were cold and unblinking, like a snake in a fridge.

"Another good man gone," he said.

"Excuse my guessing," said Daisy, "but does this little recent whitewash-and-bucket problem come as a result of a child-care . . . situation?"

"Correct," said Gomez Elegante, and something that was almost an expression flitted across his face. "My little Gomez Chico. A strong-minded, adventurous child who has difficulty relating to those less creative than himself. Also he has allergies."

Daisy allowed a thin smile to touch her lips. "And his present . . . personal assistant is psychologically trained?"

Now Gomez did look surprised. He made the sign against the evil eye and spat over his right shoulder. "Mind reader," he said. "Or maybe weetch?"

Daisy said, "Mr. Gomez, we are the answer to your problems."

"You are?" Gomez frowned. "Haven't I seen you somewhere before?"

"No," said Primrose.

"No," said Pete.

"No," said Daisy. "So where is Mrs. Gomez?"

"London?" said Gomez. "New York, Jakarta . . . Who

knows? Who cares? This time of day, the kid will be throwing martini glasses into the swimming pool—as a cry of despair, you understand. You have twenty-four hours to make heem happy again. After thees, the crocodiles."

A dark suit hustled them away.

"Where," said Daisy, "is the nursery?"

"Wha?" said the suit.

"Where do you store the kid?" said Pete.

"He has his suite," said the suit. "Right there."

They were on a patio beside a large swimming pool. Two of the picture windows looking onto the pool were boarded up with plywood, which was covered in graffiti. A small child was throwing martini glasses into the pool. He was dressed in a horrible glitter shell suit and sneakers the size of small boats. His hair was black and hung down all around his head, so his dark glasses were mere glints in the thicket.

"'ello," said Pete.

The kid did not answer.

"Good afternoon," said Daisy.

The kid threw a glass at the lip of the pool. It broke. Splinters slid into the blue waters and became invisible.

"What would you like for supper, kid?" said Primrose.

"Meat," said the kid. "Raw."

"How very nasty," said Daisy. "Primrose will make you pizza."

The kid yawned and spat.

"And you will eat it all up."

"Won't." The kid shot Daisy a glance that just about frizzled his shades.

A door opened. A middle-aged woman with white overalls and silly blue eyes came onto the pool deck. She said, "I must request that you be less judgmental with Junior." Her face was covered in sticking plaster and one of her arms was heavily bandaged.

"And who," said Pete, "might you be?"

"I am Mrs. Beek. Junior's analyst, therapist, and life mentor."

Pete said, "Had an accident, did you?"

"Cuts, bruises, a slightly broken arm. Just little Gomez Chico's rough fun, bless him," said Mrs. Beek, not meeting Pete's eye.

Primrose went up to her and took her by her good hand. "Mrs. Beek," she said, "will you come and sit with me?"

Mrs. Beek would not look at her. "Don't want to," she said.

Primrose had whipped off her bowler hat and spun it to Daisy, who hid it behind her back. "Please," said Primrose. "On this nice seat here."

When Mrs. Beek looked down, she saw a dear little girl with blond hair in an Alice band and the mildest of blue eyes. "Oh, all *right*," she said.

They sat on a swing seat, overlooking the pool.

"Excuse my saying this," said Primrose, "but I think you are not happy."

"Happy? Me?" said Mrs. Beek. "Of course . . . I . . . am . . ." She choked. A big tear slid down each side of her button nose.

"Because little Gomez is a nasty little boy."

Mrs. Beek meant to say that there was no such thing, only children whose personalities had been cramped by not getting exactly what they wanted all the time. But under the influence of Primrose's trusting blue gaze, she said, "He's a monster."

"And you have little ones of your own?"

"Yes," said Mrs. Beek.

"Where?"

"They're in prison," said Mrs. Beek, and burst into tears. "The poor mites were so frustrated at not having nice sports cars that they stole some."

"And Mr. Beek?"

"He told the children off good and proper when they burned the house down. I divorced him immediately, of course." Her handkerchief was soaked.

"There, there," said Daisy, handing the woman a hanky of her own. "Have a good blow. That's right. Now go to your room, have a shower, change your dressings, get a nice new splint, and you'll feel miles better."

Mrs. Beek bit her lip, sniffling. "I think I will," she said, and walked through a door that said COUNSELOR'S QUARTERS.

Thirty seconds later there was a mighty crash of crockery and an awful screaming.

"Oops," said Pete. "What's that?"

"Our cue to call the ambulance," said Daisy.

"What could have happened?"

"Very hard to tell," said Daisy. "But it sounded like the Black Mile."

"Sure did," said Primrose judiciously.

"Being?"

"You get some black thread from your counselor's sewing kit and you tie together all the glass and china ornaments in your counselor's room and you draw the curtains and take the lightbulb out and send the counselor in to have a shower or something. We did it to Nanny Himmler. She said it was like going mad," said Daisy. "Only perhaps a bit worse. But of course she was in a lunatic asylum, so the odds are she was exaggerating. Shall I call the ambulance or will you?"

Once Daisy had lassooed Gomez Junior and Pete had tied him up, it was quite easy to lock him in a soundproof room, of which there seemed to be a large number in the Gomez mansion.

"Well!" said Daisy. "*Not* a nice child!"

"Reminds me of myself as a lad," said Pete, picking a fingernail out of his arm.

"What next, Nanny D?" said Primrose.

"Systematic search for Papa," said Daisy.

They walked away from the soundproof room, from which now came a series of muffled thumps.

"Now, then!" said Daisy. "Scatter and report back in ten minutes. And be careful!"

Primrose muttered something about grandmothers and eggs. Off they set. After ten minutes they reassembled.

"Lot o' locked doors," said Pete.

"And no sign of Papa," said Daisy.

"Not a tweet," said Pete.

"Tweet?" said Daisy in a dangerous voice.

"Sound a bird makes," said Pete.

"Ah. Primrose?"

Primrose had her bowler hat off. She looked rather pale.

"Well?" said Daisy.

"I found this," she said, holding out a sort of whitish rag.

Pete and Daisy frowned down at the evidence. It was a pair of boxer shorts, made of the finest silk. On the name tape were written the words DARLING COLIN.

"Ah," said Daisy.

"Frankly none too clean," said Pete.

"But definitely the property of Papa," said Primrose.

There was a silence.

"What does this mean?" said Daisy eventually.

"That Papa is walking round with his bum hanging out," said Primrose.

"Quite. But where did you find them?"

"In the swimming pool changing hut. With a lot of other clothes that might have been his but did not have name tapes."

"Hmmm," said Pete.

"Significant," said Daisy.

"Wha?" said Primrose.

"Put yourself in his shoes," said Daisy.

"His shoes are in the hut."

"His . . . feet, then," said Daisy, resisting the urge to tap a brogue. "He comes down to the pool. Someone says, go on, have a swim. Don't mind if I do, he says, on account of it being hot and in the tropics, but I have left my trunks at home. Go on, borrow a pair, there are plenty in the hut, says whoever it is, Gomez Elegante, perhaps. Sharp dresser, Gomez. So Papa would have quite liked his choice of trunks. So Papa puts them on and has his swim and for some reason, like maybe someone has taken his clothes away, goes back to his room in his trunks."

"Which is well out of order," said Primrose.

"*Well* out of order," said Daisy.

"Pardon?" said Pete.

"Because, as any nanny knows, if you wear your swimsuit to your room, you drip water on the carpets and the water is full of chlorine and it makes awful bleached spots."

"Done it once, done it a thousand times," said Primrose.

"I dint know that," said Pete. "But then I never had no swimming pool nor trunks as a boy."

"But where did you *swim*?" said Daisy, appalled.

"Any big puddle, or the canal if in luxurious mood. In the nuddy."

"The nuddy. Oh, you poor dear," said Daisy. "One is so sorry for you, really, but that is quite beside the point. All we have to do is whip out a powerful lens . . . *thus*"—she pulled a magnifying glass from her pinafore pocket—"and scrutinize the carpets *thus*." She scrutinized the carpets by the doorway to the pool deck. "Aha!"

"Wha?"

"Look!"

A ghostly line of spots led along the carpet into the interior of the house.

"Could be anyone," said Pete.

Primrose had dropped to her hands and knees and was sniffing. "Still fresh," she said. "Within the past three days."

"Well, then," said Daisy. "Hats on. Quick march."

Clapping on their bowlers and straightening their shoulders, they followed the trail of spots into the interior.

It led up curling marble stairs, along beautifully carpeted passages lined with ancient Spanish doors, and down another set of stairs carved from a solid block of mahogany. It was exactly the kind of place the Darlings were used to, and it gave them a warm, homely feeling. On the ground floor they followed the hall toward the back regions of the house.

"Hist!" said Primrose after a hundred meters.

There was the sound of footsteps and voices talking in the singsong Spanish of the Gomez bodyguards. And another voice, raised and indignant.

"I can assure you that you will have my full cooperation in growing the vision," it said. "And with regard to this, I should like my trousers back."

Someone snarled something in Spanish, but Pete and the Darling girls did not even listen to what it was. For the indignant voice had been the indignant voice of Papa Darling.

A door slammed. Feet sounded. Five men walked past, hustling Papa Darling down the passage. After they had passed, a cupboard door opened, and one shaved and two bowler-hatted heads came out and watched the dark suits surrounding Papa's whitish shoulders. He seemed still to be wearing bathing trunks.

"Honestly!" said Daisy, throwing up her hands.

"After them!" hissed Pete and Primrose.

They went up more posh stairs and along more corridors. After a few lefts and rights they came out onto a sort of balcony overlooking an enormous room. Air-conditioning hummed icily. In the middle of the room was a long table. At the head of the table stood Gomez Elegante. Behind him was a huge screen showing a map that looked somehow familiar. Round the table were men in dark suits. At the foot of the table, brightly but not warmly dressed in a pair of pink-and-lime-green board shorts and many goose pimples, was Papa Darling.

"So," hissed Gomez Elegante, like a serpent, "here it is. Is there anything we should know?"

"I very much value your cooperation with regard to this venture," said Papa Darling. "It would be unhelpful to my profit share in Colossal Realty for me to hold back any relevant facts—"

"What profit share?" said Gomez Elegante.

"We are, as they say, in this together—"

"Wrong," said Gomez Elegante. "You are nothing to do with Colossal Realty. Meester Borbonski do not know this yet, but he is my partner, to spread the expenses but maybe not the profits, heh, heh. You are on your own. As you will find out when maybe we tie iron bits to your feets and drop you into nice blue sea or perhaps slather you in el mayo and feed you to ze crocs. Now, where are rocks and sandbanks?" He tapped impatiently at the map with his pointer.

Daisy, Primrose, and Pete looked at each other, eyes wide with horror and despair.

The map on the screen was a map of Skeleton Cay.

They scrutinized it in detail. It marked rocks, trees, caves, and beaches. But no X marked any spot.

"It's not the treasure map," hissed Pete. "It's a copy."

Down on the floor, Papa Darling drew himself up to his full height. "I am not at liberty to discuss these matters with any but my partners," he said.

"Tchah," said Gomez Elegante, like a snake spitting. "Take heem away."

The nannies and Pete scooted back the way they had

come, rushed into the cupboard, and had a quick, whispered planning session.

"Okay?" hissed Daisy.

"Okay!" hissed Pete and Primrose.

Out they went.

Enrico Luz was very bored to be on guard outside the cellar door. If Enrico Luz had had his way, the gringo in the swimming trunks would already have been rolled in the mayo vat and already on the truck to the crocodile swamp.

Enrico Luz was not clever enough to think inside his head. He had to say it aloud; otherwise it got muddled up. "Maybe the crocs," he was saying. "Maybe we feeds heem to, you know, beeg feesh, sharp teefs." He began to hit his head with his clenched fist to help himself remember.

"Sharks," said a voice.

"Ees right!" cried Enrico Luz. "Sharkos!" His mouth fell open. "Who you?" he said.

"A little girl who is lost," said Primrose, blinking with assumed feebleness.

"Ay," said Enrico, groping for his sheath knife, for he did not hold with little girls.

At that moment, a medium-sized asteroid smote his head and he knew no more.

"Unh," said Pete, frisking the unconscious bandit for the keys. "Here we are."

Daisy opened the door. "Papa!" she cried eagerly.

"I am in a meeting," said a voice in the darkness at the bottom of a flight of steps.

"Get him up here," said Daisy to Pete.

Pete walked down into the darkness and returned, leading Papa blinking into the light.

"Good afternoon," said Papa. "How very pleasant to renew your acquaintance. I have, however, scheduled various items for the next few hours—"

"Can it, we're scrammin'," said Pete.

"I beg your—"

But Pete was already hauling Papa down the corridor at a brisk clip.

"Wha?" cried Papa. "What are you *doing*?"

"Surging toward freedom," said Daisy.

"Surge faster!" said Primrose.

"No!" cried Papa. "You do not understand! With my associate, Mr. Gomez, I have located a most attractive development opportunity involving a resort-type destination—"

"Quite crazy," said Daisy, jogging.

"Off his head," said Primrose, keeping up.

"Listen, squire," said Pete. "You are planning to concrete over Skeleton Cay and build hotels and holiday homes, plus a fertilizer works, like. Your mucker, Gomez, has got a new partner and plans you are no part of. We heard what he said. He stole your clothes. And now he is going to lather you up with mayonnaise and feed you to the crocs, pore creeturs."

"No, no," said Papa. "He did not steal my clothes. I was called indoors from the pool and detained in proactive interface situations is all. Just his little pleasantry or joke. We are still partners. Fifty-fifty."

"So you gave Mr. Gomez the professor's note handing over the island?"

Papa Darling looked as sly as it is possible to look while running down a corridor in bathing trunks. "Only a photocopy," he said.

"Where's the original?"

"That is confidential information."

"And if you get caught by these little geezers in the dark whistles?"

"Whistles?"

"Whistles and flutes, suits."

"Ah. In the unlikely event of my demise the property passes in toto to my relicts and heirs."

They were out of the door now, running past the swimming pool. The thunder of many Cuban heels came from beyond the patio.

"Unlikely?" said Pete. "Quick! Into the nursery!"

Into the nursery they piled. The feet thundered across the patio. Fists began to hammer on the plywood shuttering that replaced the windows.

"Oi!" said a voice behind them. "'Oo you think you are?"

Standing in the shadows, wearing dark glasses, was the nasty little child known as Gomez Elegante Junior. On his wrists and ankles were the chewed remains of lashings. In his hands was a chain saw. He pulled the starting cord. The chain saw failed to start.

"'ere, my son," said Pete with a benevolent smile. "Shall I fire that up for you?"

The child turned sulky eyes on him. "Yeah," he said. "And be queek about it."

Pete took the chain saw out of the little hands and threw it away, then tossed an armchair at a small man in a dark suit who had just kicked the door down. The small man hurtled backward into the swimming pool. Pete bolted the door.

"Oi!" said the child. "You breaking promise, disappointing my expectations. Maybe I develop la trauma."

"Sorry about that," said Pete. "But what I promise you now is that you are in a hostage situation."

"'ostage?" said the child.

"Watch and you'll understand. Ready?"

"Ready," said Daisy.

"Ready," said Primrose.

Actually, neither Daisy nor Primrose was ready at all. When they had joined the burglars, it had been to teach them nanny skills and to rid their natures of dangerous softness. Getting chased by lethal suits had not been part of the deal.

It was absolutely terrifying and both of them wanted it to stop *right now*.

"Okay," said Pete. "I'll take the kid. Youse twose, stay behind me."

Eek, thought Primrose. Argh, thought Daisy. Cramming their bowler hats over their eyes and making themselves very small, they crept behind the comforting bulk of Pete.

"*Orright!*" roared Pete in a mighty voice. "*We've got the boss's kid! If you hammer us, you're hammerin' him!*"

He marched out onto the swimming pool deck. A storm of rocks, tins, bottles, and hatchets whizzed from the windows opposite. Pete and the brat did double back-somersaults.

"Don't like you much, do they?" said Pete.

"No," said the kid. "But I don' like them neither. Now, let me go, you big ox."

"What, and get you hammered?" said Pete.

Daisy found her mouth was watering.

"Nah. Where's the back door?"

"Not tellin'," said the kid.

Pete put his face—not a comforting face, if you did not know him—close to the kid's. "Tell me or perish, you little bleeder."

"Isn't one," said the kid.

"Isn't a back door?"

"Nope. There's only a silly ol' secret passage."

"Secret passage?"

"Yeah. To the airfield. So there."

"Oh," said Pete, "'ow awful. Bet you don't know where the entrance is."

"Bet I do too," said the kid.

Bricks were coming through the skylight now.

"Prove it."

The kid crawled into the back room, demonstrating a level of skill that made Daisy realize that this was quite understandably not the first time he had had sharp, heavy things thrown at him. Pete, the girls, and Papa Darling followed. The kid picked up the remote control of the huge TV and pressed buttons. The screen rolled back, revealing a flight of concrete steps leading downward.

"See?" he said.

"Most impressive," said Pete, shepherding Papa down the hole.

"What do I do now?" said the kid.

Behind them someone seemed to be bashing the nursery door in with a sledgehammer.

"You poor darling, you must come with us."

"You are total poo," said the child.

"Yes, dear," said Daisy. "Come along, dear."

Pete slung Gomez Junior over his shoulder and they ran down the steps. As the screen slid behind them, they heard the crunch of the door bursting in, the clatter of dozens of Cuban heels, and cries of frustration cut short.

"Thank goodness *that's* over," said Daisy.

"Hear, hear," said Primrose. "Biscuits for all, I think."

She passed round the tin as they trotted through the tunnel.

"Delicious!" cried Daisy.

"Quite acceptable!" said Papa Darling, crunching with the enthusiasm of one who has not been fed for days. "Though of course Mr. Elegante would have been on the point of offering me lunch—"

"Nice," said Pete. "Urgh." This last remark expressed not disgust with the biscuit but the fact that Gomez Junior had kicked him in the stomach. "Peace, child, and eat up yor bicky."

"Won't," snarled Gomez Junior, dashing bicky bits to the ground.

"Tch!" cried Daisy. "What a waste! Got any Do Right Drops, Prim?"

"Used 'em all at the airport. What we got here is just treacle cookies—"

"Taste like poo!" cried Gomez Junior. "Gimme more!"

"—which certain people will not get any more of because they are too naughty."

The walls, which had been invisible in the darkness, were going gray.

"Light at the end of the tunnel!" cried Daisy.

"Yerse, indeed!" cried Pete.

"Er . . ." said Primrose.

The light was not the end of the tunnel. It was a golf cart with its headlights on, speeding toward them.

"Leave this to me," said Daisy.

The golf cart bore down. In it were two men in the usual black suits.

"Big," said Pete.

The men were indeed big. They made Giant Luggage look like a midget. They growled extreme violence.

Daisy raised a hand. "Stop!" she cried.

The cart stopped.

"We are nannies, carrying Chico, son of Gomez Elegante," said Daisy. "We are sick of him and would like you to take him back to his papa!"

The men in black suits rumbled something in Spanish that nobody had any trouble translating as, "No way, Jose."

"In that case," said Daisy, "give us your cart."

"But—"

"Either that or take the kid."

"Have the cart!" cried the men. Leaping out, they ran for the house like gorilla-sized rabbits, their knuckles raising plumes of dust from the tunnel floor.

Daisy lashed Junior to the seat with Pete's suspenders. Then they piled in and buzzed along the tunnel, up a ramp, and out into the glaring daylight.

"My eyes!" shrieked Gomez Junior, cowering behind his hands.

"Never been outside without his shades," said Daisy. "Horrid little gangster."

The airplane was standing at the end of the runway, engines ticking over, ready for takeoff. Pete brought the golf cart alongside the cargo door.

"All aboard," said Daisy.

"Even the, er, kid?" said Papa.

"Good papas speak when spoken to," said Daisy sternly. "But since you ask, *particularly* the kid."

They all climbed aboard. The cargo hold was full of square parcels.

"Nasty smoggled stoff, I'll be bound," said Primrose.

"You and Papa throw it away, then," said Daisy severely. "I shall be at the business end."

The cockpit door was shut. Pete kicked it open. Two men in dark glasses and headphones looked round.

"Good after*noon*," said Daisy. "I do not know if you have met Gomez Elegante Junior, a.k.a. Gomez Chico? He would like to be on this flight."

The two men took one look at Gomez Junior. Then they looked at each other. Then they tore off their earphones, wrenched open a door marked EMERGENCY EXIT, and sprinted away across the white-hot runway.

"Very good," said Daisy. Then, to Junior, "Stop that!"

Junior was yanking the microphone off the radio, but nobody had ever spoken to him in that tone of voice, so he paused in his work. Swiftly Daisy lashed him to a seat. Outside the windscreen, a line of black limousines had turned onto the far end of the runway.

"Take off!" cried Daisy.

"Dunno how," said Pete.

"Oh, for goodness' *sake*!" cried Daisy. "You sit in the seat *there,* and take hold of that steering wheel thing *there,* and put your feet on those steering pedals *there,* and push those lever things *there* forward like *that*—"

"Whoa!" said Pete.

For both engines had got louder and now they were making that huge buzzing roar and the plane was rolling down the runway, faster and faster.

"What now?"

"Use your imagination!" cried Daisy. "And the steering wheel thing!"

Pete pushed the steering wheel thing away from him. The nose went down and the tail came up.

"Wrong way!" cried Daisy.

Pete pulled the steering wheel thing toward him. The nose came up and the tail went down. The line of limousines stretched across the runway like a wall of black metal. Then suddenly there was a great soft bounce and a feeling of lightness. And the limousines whipped past below, white faces in dark glasses staring up. The airplane was flying.

"Gulp," said Pete. "What now?"

"You're on your own," said Daisy. "Gangsters can do it, so burglars obviously can."

"Yeah," said Pete, gritting his teeth.

Down on the runway, most of the limousines had collided with each other. Men in black suits and dark glasses crawled out of the smoldering pile of cars. They watched as the airplane made a large, wobbly turn and headed for the horizon in a series of sickening curves.

"They've got Gomez Chico," said one of the gangsters.

"Thank goodness for that," said another of the gangsters.

The plane flew over the blue horizon and was seen no more.

"Dear me," said the captain.

Cassian steadied his telescope on a tree stump and put his eye to the eyepiece. The sea was thick with rusty hulks. They seemed to have stopped fighting and bumping into each other. Now they were plowing grooves in the pure blue water, heading straight for the island.

"What are they going to *do*?" said the captain.

"Invade," said Cassian grimly. "Pour concrete. Build."

"But it is *our* island," said the captain. "Really, this is *too* revolting."

Cassian said nothing. He was counting the men with yellow hard hats and black mustaches standing on the foredeck of the lead ship. He stopped at 110, because something was happening.

One of the ships had lowered a launch. It buzzed over the water like a rusty insect, spewing black smoke and leaving a rainbow slick of oil in its wake. It crunched into the beach and walloped a gangplank onto the sand. A fat man in a dark suit waddled down the plank and toward Cassian.

"Who is in charge here, sonny?" he said.

"Mind your own business," said Cassian, who could be extremely rude when roused.

The fat man smiled a bland, oily smile. "It *is* my bidness. Or I should say, my client's bidness. Me being a lawyer and my client being Colossal Realty, owner of this island on which you are right now trespassing."

Cassian said, "You'd better talk to the captain."

He was not very good at arguing. But he was absolutely brilliant at mechanical bits and pieces. Thanks to Dean the Wild Boy, he had a few of them in mind right now.

"Colossal Realty?" said the captain, impeccable in her dazzling white uniform. "Forgive me, but I have never heard of you. This island is our property, bought fair and square from Professor Eustace Quimby, the eminent philosopher."

The lawyer rocked a little on his heels, blinking. "Li'l lady, you are quite something," he said.

The captain raised one perfect eyebrow. "Meaning?" she said.

"Pretty li'l thing like you can't be expected to understand

the ins and outs of a property deal," said the lawyer. "So you just step aside and let the law do its—argh."

The "argh" came as a noose snaked out of the seaside vegetation, tightened round his ankles, and jerked him flat on his face in the sand.

"Gorrim," said the tiny voice of Nosy Clanger.

"Thank you *so* much," said the captain.

"Want me to fpifflicape 'im?" said Nosy, flexing fists the size of kumquats.

"Not yet," said the captain, twitching the legal paper from the fingers of the lawyer, who was now spitting sand and cursing in a most unlegal way. She frowned at the paper. "Yes," she said. "I do see that the island passed from Eustace Quimby to us. But the Papa Darling mentioned here as the partner of Gomez Elegante in Colossal Realty has of course no right to the island, having stolen the deeds—"

"Possession is nine points of the law!" spluttered the lawyer. "I have here a court order transferring ownership—"

"Quite," said the captain. "Excuse me a moment, would you?" Looking grave, she walked back up the beach. "Cassian," she said, "have you taken emergency measures?"

"Measures in place, Captain," said Cassian, saluting smartly. "All down to Dean the Wild Boy."

"In that case," said the captain, "you will please ask Dean to do his worst. And as for you, legal beagle, outies and off with you before someone gets cross."

"Can't moooffe," moaned the lawyer through a mouthful of sand.

"Soon fix that," said the captain. "Cassian?"

Cassian jumped aboard the speedboat and pointed the nose out to sea. He tied the end of the rope that was not round the lawyer's feet to the boat, locked the steering, started the engine, engaged full throttle, and stepped overboard. The speedboat hurtled toward the horizon.

"Nooo!" cried the lawyer. Then the rope round his feet snapped taut and he shot out to sea.

The captain, Cassian, and Dean the Wild Boy watched the boat whiz away, the lawyer throwing up an exciting sheet of spray in its wake.

"I wonder if he likes waterskiing," the captain said.

"Some lawyers do," said Cassian.

The speedboat hit the front ship and exploded in a gout of orange flame and black smoke. Men in hard hats rushed around with fire extinguishers. Other men in hard hats hauled the lawyer aboard.

"If only Papa Darling were here," said the captain grimly. "I'd give him lawyers."

"Look!" said Nosy Clanger, pointing. "An airplane!"

Sure enough, there, buzzing up from the south, was a tiny silver mote that grew larger and larger.

"Lookf a bip odd," said Nosy.

It did indeed. It was swerving all over the sky, up, down,

and sideways. But as far as anyone could tell, it was heading for the Colossal Realty fleet and Skeleton Cay.

"Up a bit!" cried Primrose.

The windscreen turned sky blue.

"Down a bit!" cried Daisy.

The windscreen turned sea green.

"Doin' my best," said Nanny Pete through gritted teeth.

"Faster!" said Papa Darling.

"Oh, do be quiet," said everybody else.

Far ahead, the sea was covered in ships. Beyond the ships, an island lay across the horizon.

"Skeleton Cay!" cried everybody.

The windscreen turned sky blue.

"Down—" cried Papa Darling.

"Anyone know how you land this thing?" said Nanny Pete.

Two bowler hats shook as one.

Papa Darling said, "It is simply a matter of lowering the undercarriage, engaging two degrees of flaps, throttling back to just above stalling speed, S curving into the final approach, flaring, and engaging reverse pitch the moment the tires make contact with the runway surface."

Pete Fryer pushed the steering wheel thing away from him and stood up. "You know so much, you do it," he said.

The airplane was now pointing straight down, howling toward the sea.

"Noooooo!" cried everyone, including Papa Darling.

"Mr. Fryer," cried Papa Darling, falling to his knees and clasping his hands, "please fly the plane!"

"Pretty please?"

"Pretty, pretty please!"

"'Spose," said Pete, sitting down and hauling on the steering wheel thing with the skill of twenty minutes' practice.

"Now, then," said Daisy when the plane was once more swerving normally. "Papa, I think you will have to find some parachutes. Go on."

Papa went.

"And how is Gomez Junior?" said Daisy to Gomez Junior.

Gomez Junior was still lashed to his seat. He was purple, partly with rage and partly with trying to hold his breath till he burst, just to show them. His ghastly destructive little fingers had already managed to unpick some of the upholstery and were making feeble attempts to throw it at Primrose.

"Gomez Junior, we are going to send you back to your daddy's friends."

"Don't want to go," said Gomez Junior.

"Tell that to Mr. Gravity," said Daisy, smiling sweetly and bracing herself as the plane yawed horribly across the sky. "Ah, Papa. Some parachutes, I see. Now, then, Primrose. If I untie Junior *thus,* and Papa sits on his head . . . thank you, Papa . . .

thus . . . I can put the parachute on him *thus,* and do up the buckle, and if Pete could aim for that ship, the big one over there, and we take Junior back into the cargo hold . . ."

They hauled the brat into the cargo hold. Primrose opened the door. Three hundred meters below was the rusty deck of a large ship, crowded with diggers and dozers and dumpers and concrete-making equipment.

"When you feel yourself fall, pull that ring," said Daisy, pointing to the rip cord.

"Won't!"

"All right, don't."

"Will!"

"Throw him out," said Daisy.

"Aiieeeee!" cried Gomez Junior, plummeting.

The watchers on the beach saw the little figure fall out of the airplane. They saw the parachute open. They saw it float down onto the deck of a huge, rusty merchant ship. The ones with telescopes saw the figure shake its fists, stamp its feet, kick a lifeboat, hop around the deck clutching its poor hurt toes, and go indoors. They saw the ship slew wildly sideways, as if a maniac had snatched the helm. Then they saw the ship straighten out and resume its course, as if someone had over-powered the maniac and locked it in a cupboard—

Which is to say, dear reader, that this is what they would have seen if they had been looking. But their attention was on other things. Like, for instance, the airplane from which the little figure had jumped.

The airplane was flying toward them in a series of clumsy swerves. The door in its side was open. As it approached the beach, more little figures leaped out.

First came a small girl in a gingham uniform and a bowler hat. "Geronimooooo!" she cried.

"Primrose!" cried all the burglars on the beach.

Out of the door popped another uniform and bowler hat, the brown brogues pointed stylishly in a jump of supreme elegance. "Banzaiiiiiiii!" she cried.

"Daisy!" cried all the burglars on the beach.

The next jumper was a squat, muscular figure in a dark suit. "Fulhaaaaaaaaaam!" he cried.

"Pete!" cried all the burglars on the beach.

Last out of the cargo door was a lanky man in pink-and-lime-green board shorts. "Ooh!" he said.

"Papa Darling," muttered someone, and turned away to greet the nannies and Pete, safe on the beach.

Papa Darling splashed into the sea. "Help," he cried.

"No," said someone on the beach.

Papa Darling started to swim.

Dean the Wild Boy was on the lower slopes of Skull Mountain, working with a gang of sturdy burglars, when he heard the sound of engines. He straightened from his task.

Spread across the blue sea below was the rusty red invasion fleet. Coming at him was a twin-engined airplane.

"Duck!" he cried.

A hundred sturdy burglars ducked. The airplane thundered overhead and crashed into the side of the mountain. There was a huge explosion. The ground shook.

The explosion died away. The ground did not stop shaking.

"All done here," said Dean the Wild Boy. "Maybe we should, like, go down to the beach?"

"Willingly," said the hundred burglars like one burglar.

They went down to the beach on tiptoe, paying out long strings behind them. As they went, they looked nervously over their shoulders.

The wisp of smoke rising from Skull Mountain seemed to have turned into something more like a plume.

The captain sat under a palm leaf umbrella on the terrace of Camp Civility, glancing idly at the ships and swirling a green cocktail round in her glass.

"Do you know," she said to Pete, "I think I should have a word with Papa Darling."

"What for?" said Pete.

"I wish him to conduct some negotiations."

"Where?"

"With the concrete fleet."

"Ah," said Pete, looking slightly happier. "'ere he is."

Papa Darling came in. He had found a suit somewhere. It had once been white, but someone seemed to have been cleaning floors with it. The arms were too short, the jacket too narrow.

"Papa," she said.

"Dearest Ermintrude," cried Papa, "what joy to see you safe and well!"

"Can it, Kevin."

"Colin is my new, nicer name."

"You will always be Kevin to me," said the captain, terrible in her wrath. "You are a hornswoggling crook who cannot even be trusted to clean a lavatory. You are bent as a hairpin and twistier than a plate of spaghetti and slipperier than an ice rink covered in eels. But I have a proposition for you."

"Anything," said Papa Darling over the knocking of his knees.

The captain looked at the surface of her cocktail, which was covered in little waves. "I want you to negotiate with your friends," she said. "I want you to give them the island—"

"*Give?*" said Papa Darling. "As in donate free, gratis, and for nothing, without payment?"

"Yep," said the captain. "Well, no. I want you to swap it for this ship."

The ground shuddered underfoot.

"Captain," said Cassian. "They've landed."

"Excuse me," said Papa Darling, in the voice of a man admitting defeat.

"Keep an eye on him," said the captain.

Daisy and Primrose followed their papa to the Camp Civility lavatories. They watched as he pushed open a door that said CLOSED FOR CLEANING, went to a box, and pulled out an envelope.

"Well?" he said defensively. "Where else would you hide paper, eh?"

"Dead subtle," said Daisy. "Come along, Papa."

When they got back to the captain's terrace, many ships had come ashore on the beach below—rusty, square-nosed ships that flopped ramps onto the sand. With great smoke and a throaty roar, diggers and dozers and dumpers and mixer trucks began to roll onto the beach and fan out. SWAT teams of surveyors, armed with levels and red-and-white poles, sprinted onto the sand and started marking out sites for beachfront restaurants and a four-lane highway, while elite squads of tree fellers' mates squirted red spray paint Xs on palm trees.

"Cassian?" said the captain.

"Dean the Wild Boy?" said Cassian.

Dean the Wild Boy pulled the string in his right hand.

It was a long string, one of several. It led through the coconut grove, up a valley, snaked across a cliff face, and was tied in a small but firm knot to a stick of wood that braced a medium-sized boulder overhanging the steepest part of the slope. Behind the medium-sized boulder were other boulders—many, many other boulders, in a large cone-shaped pile. It was, in short, an idea based on one of Professor Quimby's Home Landslides. But thanks to Cassian's ingenuity, the burglars' strength, and Dean the Wild Boy's local knowledge and leadership skills, it was bigger. Much bigger.

When Dean the Wild Boy pulled the string, the stick popped away from under the medium-sized boulder. The boulder started to roll down the hill. The other boulders that the first boulder had been holding up started to roll, too. They rolled slowly at first, then quicker. Some were the size of saloon cars. Others were the size of houses. They all rolled together, picking up speed as they leaped over the cliff, bouncing and leaping merrily, like great lumps of rubber.

They were not rubber, though. They were rocks. Big rocks, extremely hard and very heavy.

"Uh," said a dozer driver, pausing in his demolition of a couple of coconut palms and looking up at the doom rumbling down on him from the top of the hill. Then he said no more, for a rock bounded into his dozer blade. Machine and man sailed out to sea, landed with a complicated double splash, and were seen no more.

There was a lot of that sort of thing going on.

"That'll show 'em," said the captain, sipping. "Well *done*, Cassian."

"It was mostly Dean the Wild Boy," said Cassian, blushing a bit.

"But consider the health and safety implications!" said Papa Darling, even his suntan turning pale.

"You still here?" said the captain.

The dust blew away, but the tremor in the ground did not. From the cocktail shaker beside her came the muted jingle of ice cubes.

"Like I said," she said to Papa Darling, "it is time for you to go and negotiate. The deal is this. Mr. Borbonski is half of Colossal Realty, you say. Well, we swap the island for Mr. Borbonski's yacht, with immediate effect."

"But—"

"You got us into this," said the captain grimly. "Now you get us out of it."

Papa Darling walked away toward the landing craft nosed up on the beach. "Good afternoon," they heard him say. "Take me to your leader. I am empowered to enter into meaningful discussions vis-à-vis growing the development potentialities of this highly desirable location and drawing a line under any further activities that will tend to detract from your construction-readiness schedule."

"Wha?" said one of the surviving dozer drivers.

"Wants to see the boss," said a man with a clipboard.

"Rather him than me," said the dozer driver. "Get in that launch over there. The one with the white leather seats."

And Papa Darling, upright and self-important, climbed into the launch.

As he stepped aboard, he heard small but resolute feet behind him. He looked round. He stared.

Daisy, Cassian, and Primrose stared right back.

"You are not to be trusted on your own," said Daisy. Her brogue began to tap. "So are we going to see Gomez Elegante now, or are we waiting a week or two?"

There was a pause. The children settled on the white leather cushions.

"Forward," said Papa Darling.

The launch buzzed out over the dirty waters behind the invasion beaches and came alongside the largest of the rusty hulks. Daisy, Cassian, Primrose and Papa Darling climbed the crumbling rungs set into the side of the ship. There was a helicopter parked on deck, black, marked with the intertwined initials GE.

"Oh," said Daisy. "Gomez is here."

"Chin up," said Primrose.

"No worries," said Cassian. But he knew exactly how his older sister felt.

Small men in black suits hustled them across the blistered steel deck and into the superstructure. A door clanged behind them. The air was chilly and stank of bilge water with a hint of patchouli. The suits hustled them upstairs. Papa looked businesslike, and the children pasted on expressions of amused interest suitable for a particularly grim school trip. But in each breast beat a question, the same question, dear reader, that you will probably be asking yourself. We are in the bowels of an enemy ship, in the grip of many small men in dark suits carrying family-sized skinning knives. How in the name of goodness are we going to get out of this one?

Excellent question. Frankly, it is quite possible that getting out is not something that will happen. Happy endings are usual. But they are by no means guaranteed . . .

Excuse me. The children, Papa, and the suits are at the top of the stairs. A steel door is groaning open. On we go.

The bridge was full of sun, but Gomez Elegante had managed to find a shadow to stand in.

"Good afternoon!" cried dauntless Papa, advancing on him, hand out. "How exceptionally pleasant to renew your acquaintance. Oof," he added, colliding at stomach level with two small suits who had stepped in front of their chief.

"What you want?" said Gomez Elegante, concentrating on the nail he was filing.

"I believe that nowadays you and Mr. Property Borbonski own Colossal Realty."

"So?" said Gomez Elegante.

"Before you begin paving on this island, you will need the paper that is in my pocket."

"So I'll take eet," said Gomez Elegante, switching to a new nail.

"Only on condition that you make your partner Mr. Borbonski give us his yacht *Big Deal*."

"Why should I?" said Gomez Elegante.

"On the other hand, why shouldn't you?" said Papa Darling.

Daisy realized that for some time he had been talking in ordinary language. She feared he was getting nervous. She held her breath. Gomez Elegante might be grown up, but at bottom he was a spoiled brat. And Daisy knew from many meetings with spoiled brats that it was not sensible to appeal to their sense of reason.

Sure enough, Gomez Elegante said, "Why should I?" again.

Papa Darling seemed stumped. There was a silence.

Then Cassian said, "Because otherwise you won't get the treasure."

The Elegante eyes landed on Cassian like blobs of frozen ink. "Treasure?"

"It's on the map," said Cassian. "X marks the spot. You could have it. No need to tell Borbonski."

"And where is thees map?"

"First, you write a bit of paper," said Cassian.

The eyes did not leave him. "And what should eet say?" said Elegante, pulling out pen and notebook.

Papa Darling cleared his throat. "Heading. Without prejudice and all other matters hereinundernotwithstanding, I—"

"Try this," said Cassian. "'You can have the ship now that we have got the island and the map. Love from Colossal Realty.'"

"I love nobody," said Gomez Elegante. "I put 'yours truly,' okay?"

"'Yours truly' would be fine."

The ballpoint rumbled.

"Hand-over time," said Gomez Elegante, blowing the ink dry.

Papa pulled the paper from his pocket. Elegante held out the note. The two men swapped.

"X marks the spot, in the usual way," said Papa. "Off we go!"

The Darlings turned toward the door. Nobody else moved. The silence stretched, then sagged.

"The door?" said Papa.

"No," said Elegante, and smiled, a cold and terrible smile. He turned one eye to his chief suit. "Tie them up," he said. "Drop them in the sea. Maybe weeth some iron tied on."

"Anvils?"

"Anvils ees good. Queek, I have some treasure to fetch."

The Darling children gazed upon him, appalled. Even in

the nurseries of dukes and dictators they had never come across such behavior. Their eyes focused on the ghastly Gomez, bright and powerful as welding torches. A normal person at this point would have blushed, stammered, said the whole thing was a joke that had gone too far, and started unwrapping the lashings.

Gomez Elegante lifted his eyebrow a millimeter. "So I should blush and stammer and say, ees a joke and all that?" he said. "Bot is not a joke. So get ready to say to Meester Feesh, hi, we ees breakfast."

"Gulp," said Primrose as the suits tied the Darlings to anvils.

"Hear, hear," said Daisy as the suits carried the Darlings onto the deck.

"Hmmm," said Cassian as he tested the last knot and found it 100 percent escape-proof, like all the others.

"Uh-oh," said Papa as it sank in that things were not going very well.

"*Vamonos,*" said Gomez Elegante, waving his thin cigar at the turbid waters twenty meters below.

Reader, there is no way out of this. The nearest friendly face is two miles away. Daisy, Primrose, Cassian, and their papa are fish food for sure. There is no chance of last-minute rescue, because Gomez Elegante is cruel and inflexible and no fun at all.

Dark-suited arms lifted the Darlings onto the rail.

"*Va—*" said Gomez Elegante.

The door burst open. "*Eeeeeeeeeeeeeeey!*" shouted a voice like bad chalk on a worse blackboard. "Wha you doin'?"

"Trowin' the bad guys inna sea," said Gomez Elegante to his son.

"Don' do it!" cried Gomez Junior. "Don' *do* it!"

"Wha?" said the indulgent father. Then, impatiently, "Put 'em down, guys. You hear what Gomez Chico say."

There were sulky mutterings, but the suits laid the Darlings on the deck.

"So, you wanna take 'em to the kitchens, Chico, feed 'em inna enchilada machine?"

"Noooooooooooooooooooo!" bellowed Gomez Chico. "They *cool*!"

"Wha?" said just about everybody, including the Darlings.

"They ees cruel but fair," said Gomez Chico. "They no throw things. They give me cookie. Also, when they throw me out of plane, they show me where is reep cord. I like 'em. I wanna *live* with 'em."

"You heard what the man said," said Primrose to the nearest suit. "Heave-ho."

"*¿Qué?*"

"Throw us overboard," said Daisy.

"Me first," said Cassian.

Instead their bonds were cut and they were set on their legs and dusted off.

"Of course," said Gomez Elegante, "you take sheep that I have given you, you cannot take my sweet leetle Gomez Chico, the happle of my eye—"

"*Wanna!*" roared Gomez Chico.

Gomez Elegante swayed his snake head close to Papa and said, "Get out of here before I change my mind."

The Darlings got out.

In the boat back to the beach, Papa Darling said, "How did you do it, Primrose?"

"Me?" said Primrose.

"I have heard that you make, ahem, concoctions with a view to changing the psychological outlook of the consumer," said Papa Darling. "Sleepy Cake. Do Right Drops. That kind of thing. But how did you get them to Gomez Chico?"

"Didn't," said Primrose.

"Wha?"

"Force of personality needs no medicine," said Daisy.

"Catch him!" cried Cassian.

For Papa Darling had fainted dead away.

Ten minutes later they sat on the bridge of the *Big Deal*, now officially the *Kleptomanic II*, sipping delicious ice-cream sodas and burrowing their toes into the white silk carpets.

"I quite liked the island," said Primrose, gazing at the bulldozers creeping up Skull Mountain. She frowned. "I thought everybody was off it."

"They are."

"But it looks as if someone is having a barbecue at the top."

"A barbecue?"

"Look." She pointed.

And sure enough, on the bald summit of Skull Mountain the plume of smoke had become more of a column.

"Big fire," said Daisy.

"Whatever they are cooking will certainly get burnt," said Primrose.

"I don't think it's that kind of fire," said Cassian. "Look at the coconuts."

They looked at the coconuts. All along the shore, the trees were behaving in a most peculiar way, as if someone had taught them to dance the shimmy. Coconuts were raining onto the sand. From the crocodile swamp, long, gnarled shapes were paddling out to sea, looking nervously over their shoulders. The air was full of a deep, throbbing rumble.

"Most impressive," said Daisy, who, now that all the fuss seemed to be over, was longing to stretch out on a nice sandy beach and start a really splendid tan. "Can't we have a swim?"

"There is a perfectly good swimming pool on B deck," said the captain. "This is not a sensible place to be swimming just now."

"The crocodiles," said Primrose.

Dean the Wild Boy whispered something in her ear.

"No way," she said.

"Way," said Dean the Wild Boy.

"And you knew all along?"

Dean the Wild Boy shuffled his feet.

"Knew what?" said Daisy.

Nobody answered. They all looked at the thickening column of smoke pouring from Skull Mountain.

"It looks to me," said the captain finally, "as if this island might be slightly unstable in spots."

"Yes, indeed," said Dean the Wild Boy.

"But your grandpa *sold* it to us," said Daisy indignantly. "Knowing about Gomez Elegante. And knowing about . . . this!"

"He had to sell it to somebody."

"How true," said Primrose.

"I understand perfectly," said Daisy.

Which is more, dear reader, than you do. Wait, though. Be patient. All will become clear.

The engine room was spick-and-span, except for the control booth in the corner, where the chief had installed his collection of cuckoo clocks and other memorabilia. Cassian knocked on the booth door.

There was no answer.

Cassian pushed the door open.

There was no chief.

Cassian pondered for a moment. Then he picked up the telephone and dialed the bridge.

"Up anchor," said the captain.

"Er . . ." said Pete Fryer, putting the phone down.

"What is it?" said the captain, who always had time for Pete.

Pete pointed over the side. A small figure in a white uniform cap was swimming furiously toward the beach, zigzagging between crocs. "Isn't that Cassian?" he said, in the voice of one who knew perfectly well who it was but did not want to cause trouble.

The captain sighed. "So it is," she said. "Avast."

"Pardon?"

"Belay. Oh, for goodness' sake, don't pull up the dratted anchor. We're staying put for the moment. And someone please lower a boat."

There was a silence, broken only by the thunder of coconuts on the beach. Nobody had ever seen the captain so miffed.

Things must be getting serious, no error.

Cassian's feet touched ground. Picking up a giant conch shell from the high-tide mark, he crammed it over his ears. A crocodile snapped at his heels, but he paid it no attention. Coconuts drummed on the shell as he rushed through the trees. The ground rose in front of him, shuddering. Stones bounced down the hill, and the earth and rock underfoot quivered like the skin of an animal. Bulldozers were roaring to and fro. By the smell of rotten fish, he was getting near the chief's palaces, but it was hot and the shuddering of the island made seeing difficult. After a couple of minutes he heard a strange sound. If he had not known, he would have said that it was a Swiss yodeler complaining of a slightly broken leg, having fallen down the Matterhorn. But he had heard it before, on evenings when Primrose had cooked salt cod for dinner and sent it down to the engine room of the old *Kleptomanic*.

It was Chief Engineer Crown Prince Beowulf of Iceland (deposed), and he was singing of home.

The air began to stink of rotten fish. Dashing the sweat from his eyes, Cassian found himself standing outside the door of the larger of the two wooden palaces. The singing seemed to be coming from inside. Straightening his collar (the chief was fussy about such matters), he marched on.

The house was full of smoke. At first Cassian thought it was on fire. But this smoke smelt strangely of sulfur. And it seemed to be mixed with a lot of steam, too.

> "Ach shcrubadubdub
> ve rub and ve scrub
> und ze lava goes flub
> down in ze earth's hub!"

wailed the great voice of the chief.

It was coming from a door in the wall opposite. The *solid rock* wall opposite.

Cassian wiped a hand across his sooty forehead. Then he twisted the door handle and went in.

He was in a passage that led into the heart of the mountain. There were naked lightbulbs overhead, flickering in time to the shudder of the rock.

"Oooooooooh," cried the voice. "Magma, magma,
give me your lava, do!
Here I am in
ze bath wiz I bet you know who!"

Splendid harnessing of geothermal energy, thought Cassian, trotting down half a mile of tunnel. At the end, he trotted round a corner.

And stopped.

He had found the treasure of Deathboy Ingleby.

The passage had widened out into a cave. All round the rough-hewn walls were chests, some of which had burst, releasing floods of gold coins. In the middle of the cave was a large bathtub. In the bathtub, paying no attention to the billions in gold that tiled his walls, sat Chief Engineer Crown Prince Beowulf of Iceland (deposed). He was scrubbing himself with a large brush. Wedged among the complicated taps and pipework by his feet was the teddy bear known as the Royal Edward.

"Ahem," said Cassian.

The singing stopped. From behind the rock came a rumbling. Pieces of eight clinked and the bath rocked slightly on its lion feet. The head turned. The nose was ten centimeters long, the eyes whirling below the spiked helmet on the pear-shaped head.

"Come on in!" howled the chief. "Ze water's lovely!"

"Not just at the moment," said Cassian. His heart had sunk. The mountain was now actually jumping about. And here was the chief, quite definitely Off on One. "We must go. And don't let the bath out."

"*Nonsense!*" roared the chief. "Now is wolcanic bath fitted with heat exchanger and I am singing to Edvard in the schteam! *Nicht wahr*, Edvard?" he cried, waving to the bear.

The bear remained silent.

Cassian would have been surprised if it had done anything else. But it had given him an idea. "Oh, well," he said. "Ship's leaving."

"Let it leave!" howled the chief. "See how far it gets mitout—oi!"

For Cassian had darted forward, seized the Royal Edward from its vantage point among the taps, and sprinted back up the passage.

"Nooooooo!" cried a great Icelandic voice.

There was the sound of a huge body getting out of a huge bath. Huge wet feet slapped the rock of the corridor. Cassian shot through the palace and burst into the air. There seemed to be bulldozers everywhere. He waited until the palace door flew open, and the chief stood there, vast and lard-colored, dressed only in a small bath towel and a spiked helmet, with (Cassian noted grimly) a bath plug in his hand.

"Come and get me!" said Cassian, making the Royal Edward wave a tiny paw.

"*Kill!*" roared the chief.

Cassian took off. The ground was going up and down like a trampoline as he sprinted down into the coconut groves. He found his conch shell, jammed it on his head, and ran onto the beach.

The *Polite Children* was waiting, gangplank down. Primrose was sitting in the stern. He threw her the Edward and ran up the gangplank just as the chief thundered out of the trees with a coconut stuck on his helmet spike.

"*Kill* them *all!*" he roared.

"Hmmm," said a nearby dozer driver. "Nice idea."

But the chief had rushed up the gangplank and was advancing on Cassian, his large, mad, royal hands clenching and unclenching.

"Hey!" said Primrose, dangling the Royal Edward over the boat's propeller. "One step nearer and the bear gets it."

The boat drew away from the beach.

"Catch," said Primrose, and threw the stuffed bed creature at the chief.

"*Velcom home!*" roared the chief, folding the bear in his arms and beginning to blubber and mumble in a frankly disgusting manner.

"Back to the ship," said Cassian.

"My *hero*!" breathed Primrose, taking his hand.

"Ugh," said Cassian.

"Sorry," said Primrose. "Thought you'd like it."

As the launch steamed back to the *Kleptomanic II*, a helicopter landed on the beach. Gomez Elegante got out and walked ashore. It looked as if his merciful mood had not lasted very well.

"He's won," said Primrose gloomily.

"For the moment," said Cassian.

A small figure rushed out of the helicopter and threw sand in Gomez Elegante's eyes. Gomez Elegante drew a gun. The small figure backed off with its hands up.

"It is always pleasant to see a father and son playing happily together," said Cassian.

The launch came alongside the *Kleptomanic II*. Great hooks descended and lifted it on deck. Daisy was there, cool and elegant, and the captain, and Giant Luggage, who took the coconut off the chief's helmet spike, wrapped him and the Edward in a bathrobe, and led them away.

"So *what* was that all about?" said the captain.

"He misses Iceland very much," said Cassian.

"Poor chief," said Daisy

Cassian said, "We'd better get the anchor up, by the way. Yes, poor chief, he loves the old ways. But it was all so long ago now, he can't even remember how to dry a codfish properly."

"Or we would have found the treasure," said Dean the Wild Boy. "And now Gomez Elegante has it."

"Not for long," said Cassian.

"There, there," said Primrose.

"Full ahead, both," said the captain.

The *Kleptomanic II* turned toward the open sea and began to slide rapidly through the water.

The bulldozers were crawling over Skeleton Cay like flies on a pie. Most of the coconut groves were already down, and concrete trucks trundled along the beach past Gomez Elegante, who was making exceptionally rude signs at the departing *Kleptomanic II*.

"There goes Camp Civility," said Daisy as the dozers tore into the facade. "Oh, dear, I do hate losing."

"He who laughs longest laughs last," said Cassian.

"That is a very nanny thing to say."

"It is also true."

Daisy opened her mouth to say something optimistic. Her mouth stayed open, but no sound came out. For at that moment, the top blew off Skull Mountain.

"Oh," said everyone on the *Kleptomanic II*'s bridge.

Reader, you have probably seen it coming. The wisp of smoke from the right eye of the skull, for instance. The way the smoke turned from a wisp to a plume to a column. The way the ground had been shaking for the past few hours. The way (we have not described this so far, but better late than never) that the whole island had risen thirty-eight-point-nine centimeters in the last week.

Anyway.

The top blew off Skull Mountain. Then from the bowels of the planet there hurtled a pillar of fire, accompanied by lava—both fluid and sticky, pyroclastic flows, and clouds of ash and pumice (geography). Boiling rock flooded into the sea. Mountains of steam rose into the stratosphere and became cumulonimbus laced with lightning (meteorology). There was a bang that drove the eardrums together in the middle of the head (bit of an exaggeration). Skeleton Cay, the building materials ships of Colossal Realty, and the evil Gomez Elegante vanished into a huge white mound of vapor and were never seen again. Not by those on board the *Kleptomanic II*, certainly.

"Goodness, a volcano," said Daisy.

"Explosive type," said Primrose, who excelled at geography.

"Hold tight," said the captain as a medium-sized tsunami rolled under the *Kleptomanic II*. "Cassian, are you responsible for this?"

"Act of nature," said Cassian.

"Come *on*," said the captain, Primrose, Daisy, and Pete all together.

Cassian shrugged. "And the chief's bath," he said.

"Wha?"

"It is a matter of superheat water-vapor pressure differentials and—"

"Come again?" said Pete.

Cassian sighed. "The chief is a brilliant engineer," he said. "But he has lost his grip on Icelandic skills. The dried cod we have already touched on. Well, he recognized that the cay was somewhat volcanic. So he made himself a volcano bath, like the volcano baths of his dear lost childhood—a reservoir of water, superheated by lava and very refreshing too. But he failed to arrange for appropriate gray water disposal—"

"Cassian!" said Daisy, in a voice like a whiplash.

"Which is to say, he let the bathwater out into the volcano. Where it touched the lava. And exploded. And set off a chain reaction of explosions that flattened the island."

There was a silence, except for the roar and bubble of the now distant volcano.

Finally Daisy said, "There is a perfectly good sauna on this ship."

"He is already in it," said Primrose.

"Good. Well," said the captain, "pity about the treasure, but we have a new ship with state-of-the-art everything. All's well that ends well."

She shaded her eyes with an elegant hand, gazing across the water to the clear blue horizon ahead.

Into the silence came a whistling. A man walked past. He

wore large black rubber gloves. He carried a mop in one hand and a bucket in the other. He smiled nervously. "Where are we going now?" he said.

"You," said the captain, "are going to start at the bottom. Or, in this case, the forward lower deck lavatories. The ship's cat has just been sick there and it needs cleaning up, chop chop."

"Yes, dear," said Papa Darling, and clanked off.

"Well," said the captain. "A film in the ship's cinema? Bowling in the ship's alley?"

Daisy drew herself up to her full height. "Captain, we were not put on earth to amuse ourselves," she said. "Fun in the sun is all very well, and it is highly creditable to have nicked a ship this big and luxurious. But we must not turn our backs on the basics. I suggest burgling drill and nanny skills."

"Hear, hear," said Cassian, Primrose, and Pete.

A smile of pure affection spread over the captain's lovely face. "Darlings, *darlings*," she cried. "You are so right, as always! Burgling drill it is!"

And the *Kleptomanic II* sailed elegantly in the general direction of the sunset.